MOSTLY MURDER

A Medley of Mayhem & Mystery

By

Gioya McRae

Publisher's Note

This collection is a work of fiction. Names, characters, places, and incidents are either the product of the author's imagination or are used fictitiously, and any resemblance to actual persons, living or dead, or locales is entirely coincidental.

For information address:
Mocha Mind Communications
76 McKay Ave, Suite 101, East Orange, NJ 07018.
www.mochamind.com
info@mochamind.com

ISBN 0-9774542-0-7

Published by Mocha Mind Communications

Printed in the USA

DEDICATION

This book is dedicated to my mother, Gloria, who taught me to define my own expectations and not live by others' limits.

CONTENTS

INTRODUCTION

When I began seriously writing, I felt a need to be the next Maya Angelou, Susan Taylor or Iyanla Vanzant. Guilt burdened me, because although my soul held many stories of spiritual growth, I loved to read and write mysteries. Many writers of color feel pigeon-holed into expressing themselves along political or social lines only. It is our duty to educate and prepare the next generation for the actualities of the world they have entered. But my longing to write "strange" stories lingered and grew inside me.

Why should we limit ourselves to one venue? We are individuals. We should not be one small African-American section in the bookstore. Our generous works should be spread throughout all categories, as are our minds. Yes, it is important to educate our people politically, socially, economically. There are many people of color who do just that. But maybe my role is to show by example another venue for our talents.

"Mostly Murder" shows serious, humorous, and mysterious sides of my mind. Don't be ashamed to let both your left *and* right brains indulge themselves. Free your mind and soul.

Character cannot be developed in ease and quiet. Only through experience of trial and suffering can the soul be strengthened, ambition inspired, and success achieved.

Helen Keller
US blind & deaf educator (1880 - 1968)

PRINCE OF THE PARKING LOT

Brian Palmer frowned inside, but outwardly kept his calm demeanor. It wasn't the first time Burdon had reamed him out over nothing. Even the closed frosted glass door couldn't keep the loud voices from leaking into the press room. The other reporters didn't even have to tilt their heads for clearer hearing. So they were able to appear as though they were working as usual.

Brian Palmer had been a reporter for the Star-Time Press for five years; Ned Burdon had been the Editor for only two. But those were the two most miserable years Brian had experienced in his lifetime.

"I just misplaced one piece of documentation. The story is legit. Why do you put me through this with every submission?"

"Because you shouldn't be here! Your stories put this paper in jeopardy whenever they can't be verified. Crawford would have fired you if he hadn't died of a heart attack."

Brian pounded his large, brown fists on Burdon's desk, splashing his ever-present cup of java. "Stop hounding me! You know Mr. Crawford was like a father to me."

"Don't you play that card with me. Charlie and I go way back, before you knew how to read and write," Burdon snarled. "Now you back up this story properly or it's out!"

Brian's false story was printed five years ago when he started out as a cub reporter. Mr. Crawford, the editor at the time, had taken a liking to Brian and taken him under his wing. Rumors of favoritism spawned jealousies. Brian fought daily to prove himself to coworkers and management.

Then in a spurt of misjudgment Brian fabricated a story, not just a story, but an amazing tale of intrigue, larceny, and greed. Crawford was so taken with the article, he printed it on faith.

The item cause quite a stir, fueling requests for reprints and further information. When the Newark Police Fraud Department, contacted Mr. Crawford for details, he stood proudly with his arm around Brian's shoulder and stated, "We cannot disclose our sources."

After much wrangling, the police left in a huff, averring their quick return with subpoenas.

Once alone with Mr. Crawford, Brian had crumpled into a chair and tearfully revealed the story was false from start to finish. He could almost see his beloved editor shrink as he spoke. Crawford sat limply in his leather high back chair and hung his head in silence for a full fifteen minutes. Then, one by one, he called the police chief and his competitors who had purchased reprint rights, and apologized profusely.

Retractions flew from all papers. The Star-Time Press' retraction was short, sweet and very humble. The competition's retractions were explosive attacks on Star-Time, Mr. Crawford, and Brian. Resisting great pressure to fire Brian, Crawford kept him on, although on a very short leash. He rightly saw the blunder as a rookie's attempt to defend himself from accusations of partiality. After all, wasn't he partly to blame?

Crawford was never the same after that. His health slowly deteriorated, until one day, in a heated discussion with management about one of Brian's pieces, he grabbed his chest, and keeled over. He died before reaching the hospital.

Brian's world crumbled.

Ned Burdon took over as Editor. You would have thought the job description included *"Get rid of Brian Palmer"*. Burdon made Brian's life a living hell from day one.

Ned Burdon was a wealthy man who loved playing

Editor. He blue-penciled even the most well written stories fervently. Even though he had a luxurious home in West Orange, occupied by a beautiful young wife, he kept an apartment close to the office so he could wield his power 24/7.

He personally funded special golf outings for his hand picked reporters, making sure to snub Brian. He even extended his Florida time-share to the staff members he liked.

Brian was miserable, but unfortunately, no other paper would take him after his notoriety. He was stuck. All he had ever wanted was be a reporter. His heart did not allow him another choice.

After another of Burdon's tongue lashings, Brian needed to calm his nerves. He pulled into the parking lot of Leaking Liquors, aptly named for the number of thefts which occurred from the store. Located on one corner of a decaying intersection, it was a seedy establishment with dirty windows, the obligatory neon signs declaring "Wine, Liquor, and Beer" blinking erratically, filthy cracked tile floors, and a beat up counter where a loaded forty-five was now stored.

The other corners were just as shabbily occupied. A no name gas station sat directly across from the liquor store. It had the nerve to sport a half empty clothing dumpster with a torn DARE sticker on the front. The infrequent donors who risked stopping there to drop off clothes had little worth wearing, and those clothes were stolen before DARE could empty the bin. The Middle-Eastern gas station owners closed at 7pm every night and got out of Dodge before nightfall.

The corner diagonally across from Leaking Liquors was occupied by a burned out house. It had fallen apart piece by piece since the fire five years ago. There wasn't even enough of a structure for the drug addicts to sleep in. The property owner had long abandoned it, and the city was taking action against him to no avail.

The final corner was an empty grass lot. Even though it was fenced in with chicken wire, people had dumped everything from fast food containers to kitchen sinks there. The city sign "No dumping under penalty of law" was laughable.

Brian stopped at Leaking Liquors regularly on his way home after a harrowing day at the office. He hopped out of his 1998 Toyota 4 Runner in anticipation of a cold Bud Light. As he turned to shut his car door, a flurry of movement flashed in the corner of his eye. Turning quickly, Brian spotted what he thought was a large dog moving toward the back of the building. Brian laughed at his reaction and went inside to buy his beer.

Back at his car, he fumbled for his keys. Again, movement. Brian put the cold beer on the floor of his car, so the moisture wouldn't wet the seats and walked cautiously to the back of the building. The lot was closed in by solid wood panel fencing. One dim light partially lit the area from the rooftop. An ancient, grimy dumpster reeking of stale liquor was pushed clumsily against the back of the building. The houses which abutted the fence on the either side were abandoned and boarded up long ago. Brian thought *I must be crazy. If I get hurt back here, no one will even see me.*

He stopped and listened. No sound. As he turned to leave, he heard a muffled groan. He tiptoed around to the other side of the dumpster to find an old bearded man crouching in the corner, covered with newspaper. Ironically, it was the Star-Time Press.

"Are you all right, Mister?" Brian asked from a safe distance. He was still unsure of his safety.

The man just groaned and rustled the papers closer to his chin.

"What's your name? Do you have a home? Do you need some help?" Brian moved into reporter mode.

"What are you doing back here? Do you live here?"

In response to an elongated silence, Brian started back to his car.

"Malachi," a raspy voice replied.

Brian spun back to face the withered figure. "What?"

"Malachi Walker is my name."

Brian stepped into the shadowed corner, encouraged by the reply.

Malachi stuck out a dirty hand and said, "Can you spare a couple of bucks for some food?"

This request had become more common over the years as sections of the city went to seed. Brian had long ago stopped giving money to strangers. There were too many hustlers on the streets these days. If the person looked really down and out, Brian would take him to the nearest food establishment and buy him a meal. If the panhandler refused the offer, Brian knew he was a fake.

Bone weary and ready to go home, Brian made the offer he knew would be refused.

Malachi pushed against the brick wall for leverage and stood up shakily. "Let's go."

They took a quick ride to the local diner on Main Street. It was a landmark in the city due to their good food and varied menu. They might have been refused entry due to Malachi's appearance, but the place was nearly empty so the hostess reluctantly allowed them to take a booth in the back.

Brian watched in wonder as Malachi slurped down a large bowl of vegetable soup, devoured a cheeseburger and fries, and gulped three cups of steaming hot coffee without stopping for breath.

Malachi burped loudly in contentment; then looked Brian intently in the eyes. "You're a reporter. Aren't you?"

Brian's eyes widened. "How did you know?"

"Because I used to be a reporter, just like you."

"Oh really?" Brian smirked unbelievingly. "For what paper?"

"The Headline News. I used to write under a pen name. I was the best reporter they had." Malachi looked past Brian wistfully.

"Why did you stop being a reporter?"

"It wasn't by choice." In the next hour Malachi laid out a tale of the misdeeds of the Headline News's senior editors and how, as punishment for threatening to break their code of silence, Malachi was ostracized and eventually fired from his position. He was blackballed from the writing profession and subsequently, lost his family and home. As with most people, he was only a few paychecks away from sleeping in the streets. "That's my story," Malachi shrugged.

The waitress dropped the check on the table and signaled Brian to leave by looking deeply into his eyes.

Once outside, Brian and Malachi amiably parted ways. Malachi stumbled down Main Street burping loudly every few steps.

Brian shook his head. *Well, at least he was an entertaining drunk.*

That night Brian tossed in his bed. His mind flipped back and forth through the pages of Malachi's story. *It would make a great article, if it were true.* He rolled out of bed and turned on his Dell computer. He had a fast cable modem internet connection and soon Googled the Headline News.

It was a defunct paper that closed its doors twenty years prior. *Could he be telling the truth?* There were no archived articles online. Brian would have to check microfiche files at the Newark Library for more information.

As Brian unsuccessfully surfed the internet for information, his adrenaline began to churn. He smelled a story…no an epic!

The next morning Brian awoke early feeling a vague feeling of urgency. He left a voice mail message for Burdon that he would be working from home on a new story. He was waiting at the Newark Library's doors when they opened at 9am. He had scanned the tattered microfiche files looking for articles by Malachi Walker. He searched for two hours before remembering that Malachi had said he wrote under a pen name. Brian was about to switch off the microfiche machine in disgust when an article caught his eye.

Under great duress, Headline News Editor, Charles Crawford, released a statement that journalist Jonas Walker had been writing false stories. It was with great regret he fired Walker. He apologized to the public for this shoddy and unprofessional behavior. Then he, himself, stepped down as Editor.

There was a grainy photograph of the two men leaving the Headline News building. Brian couldn't see either face clearly enough for identification, even when he zoomed in. He printed the article and ran out the door, leaving the microfiche humming.

Back at home Brian pulled out the microfiche printouts. One article was located on page two, the page which reflected the special sections and the principles' names. The Headline News had only three editors, the chief editor, Charles Crawford and two junior editors. Prominently noted under Crawford's name were the junior editors, Melinda Menace and Ned Burdon!

Brian sat stunned holding his coffee cup mid-air. A flood of adrenaline and relief rushed his system at once. This story was his chance for so many things. He could restore his position at the Star Times. He could work in peace. He could be eligible for high profile stories again. But most of all, he could get Burdon.

It all made sense now. Brian's jumbled thoughts

crystallized. The dead reporters, the missing money. If he could connect everything to Burdon, his troubles would be over.

Brian pulled into the Leaking Liquors parking lot. It looked even dirtier in the sunlight. He ran around to the back of the dumpster to find only crumpled bits of a Star-Time Press newspaper rustling in the morning breezes. There was no Malachi in sight.

Brian walked inside the fluorescent lit liquor store. The small Asian man behind the counter gave Brian a quick appraising glance and went back to reading his newspaper. He looked as though he hated being in his own store, but would snatch your money as soon as you offered it and slam your change down on the counter, ignoring your open hand. Despite his rudeness he was guaranteed business on this seedy corner.

Brian disturbed the counterman's library time, "I'm looking for the old man who sleeps in back of this store."

The Asian man looked at Brian as if he had two heads. "Sleep behind store? Nobody sleep behind store. I lock fence every night." He submerged his head behind the newsprint again.

"There is an old man with a gray beard and raggedy clothes. He was in this parking lot last night."

With an exaggerated sigh, the Asian slammed his paper down on the counter. "Nobody sleep behind store! Buy something or get out!" He didn't bother to pick up his paper again until Brian left.

Brian crossed the street to the gas station.

A thin, sandy haired, light skinned man emerged from the grimy office. "Yes?" he said with a Spanish accent.

"I'm looking for an old man with a beard who sleeps in back of the liquor store. Have you seen him?"

Apparently, the only word gas man understood was "liquor". "Across street." He pointed to Leaking Liquors.

Patiently as possible, Brian tried again, "I know that. I'm looking for a man…"

The confused look on the station manager's face told Brian to stop right there. He thanked the man and walked back to his car muttering, "I've got to learn to speak Spanish." Brian often wavered between wishing gas station attendants would learn to speak English and wishing he had learned another language.

He stood there, hands on hips, searching the seedy scenery for signs of life. The houses that were occupied had the blinds shut. In this neighborhood, you didn't want anyone looking inside your home to see what you had, even if it wasn't much.

Later that evening Brian returned to the parking lot on the hunch that Malachi only came around at night. A bunch of teen boys wearing doo rags and braids postured on the corner. Baggy jeans hung below their hipbones, exposing their underwear and long, white tee shirts hung from their muscular builds. Someone was making a killing on white tees.

Brian walked into the dark lot, craning his neck to see around the dumpster, before going back there. He could just make out a crumpled mound of newspapers sprouting wild grey hairs from the top.

"Malachi, is that you?" Brian asked as if it could be anyone else.

Startled, Malachi popped his head out of the paper pile and looked around fearfully. Once he focused his eyes on Brian, he relaxed. "Oh, it's you. Are we going to the diner again?"

Brian laughed both at Malachi's reaction and in relief. "Are you hungry?"

They took the same back booth in the diner. This

time Brian was prepared.

"What was your pen name?"

"Jonas Walker"

Pay dirt! Brian smiled.

In the next hour Malachi explained, "Local politicians paid the editors boo-koo money for favorable, promotional articles about themselves and paid even more to dishonor their opponents. The editors paid a cut of that money to a hand-picked group of reporters to do the actual writing."

Brian stopped scribbling long enough to ask, "Why didn't you take the money?"

Malachi looked him in the eye and said, "I'm just not that kinda guy. Don't you know *any* honest people, man?"

Brian continued to interrogate Malachi until he had enough details to begin his story. Before they parted company, Brian asked, "Where can I find you?"

Malachi had already started up Main Street. He shrugged, "Around."

That night in his bed, Brian tossed uncontrollably. He held a masterful story of intrigue and corruption with political ties, but could he keep Mr. Crawford's reputation clean? He owed him that much.

In the morning Brian begged his way into a short leave of absence to work on a personal story. He promised the biggest blockbuster story of the year. In truth, Burdon let him go just to keep him out of the newsroom.

Back in the Newark Library, he scanned the microfiche files to copy the stories that Malachi said were false and paid for. They were all first or second page stories. He printed copies of the articles, made note of the bylines and went home to do his internet follow up.

At home he was able to Google many of the sullied reporters by name. He came up with hundreds of articles by them, enough to keep his printer humming all night. He planned to speak to each reporter separately. In preparation for the meetings he searched for bios of each correspondent.

The first, Samuel "Silky" Darden, known for his ability to infiltrate gangs with his slick lingo and funky appearance, died in a motorcycle accident fifteen years ago. The next, Adam Angler, a tough, no holds barred journalist was killed in a barroom brawl. The third newshound was found drowned in his bathtub, an accidental death caused when his radio fell off a shelf into the soapy water.

One by one Brian uncovered the deaths of each reporter slated for his interview. By the end of his search, he sat shaken and sweating, wishing for a case of Rheingold instead of a six pack of Bud Light.

Standing in the darkened livingroom of his modest house staring unseeing into the street, Brian gripped a cold brew in his meaty fist. Misty thoughts of dead reporters wafted through his brain. This was a big story, bigger than he'd ever written. Separately, each death seemed plausible, but together they formed a clear picture of horror. One question thundered in Brian's mind. *Why is Malachi still alive?*

Brian strolled out onto his front porch and allowed the beer to cool his nerves, he spotted a lone figure standing in the shadows across the street. He leaned on the railings and squinted to get a better look. The man stumbled down the street. *Just a drunk.*

That morning, wavering between reluctance and excitement, Brian called Ned Burdon and pitched his story. Burdon was silent for a few moments after Brian finished. Just as Brian was going to break the silence, Burdon spoke.

"Are you crazy? You want to sully the names of great news people on the word of a drunken bum? Is this how you repay Charles Crawford? I told him you weren't worth his time! If this is how you're spending your leave of absence, you need to get your ass back to the newsroom."

Brian had feared this reaction. "I'm gathering proof as we speak."

"What kind of proof? You better be damned sure of this piece, or it's the end of your career!" Burdon slammed the phone down before Brian could answer.

Brian headed out to the diner for his usual breakfast of steaming coffee, scrambled eggs with cheese, grits, and beef sausage. He took the same booth he and Malachi had shared. As he waited for his meal, he jotted down items he wanted to research for his career-breaking lead story.

There were only a few diners this morning as the morning rush had passed. An old woman sipped tea and munched her whole wheat toast quietly. A policeman was picking up a take out order from the counter. A man sat in a corner booth mostly hidden behind the morning edition of the Star-Time. Cigarette smoke rose above the newspaper, and Brian wondered how he flicked the ashes without putting the paper down.

I'll start by talking to the families of the dead newsmen

The trip to Long Valley was a soothing ride up Route 80 west. Windows down; radio off. Brian had a chance to clear his head. He was visiting Silky Darden's only living kin, his sister.

Brian pulled his well-worn Toyota into the driveway, blocking in a shiny blue Lexus LS. He had called ahead and was expected. A forty year old, ash blonde woman wearing Prada jeans and a pink, silk, Gucci shell emerged from the front door of her large modular home. The entire area had a fresh garden smell about it.

Brian extended his hand, "Hello Mrs. Raymonde. I'm Brian Palmer. Thanks for agreeing to see me."

She ushered him onto her enclosed front porch where she had a pitcher of lemonade and two glasses waiting. Brian sat carefully in one of the white rattan chairs. Mrs. Raymonde hadn't smiled yet. She was still cautiously studying Brian.

Finally, she broke the awkward silence, "I always thought there was something suspicious about Sam's death. Sam had been riding that motorcycle for years without incident. The police said he hit an oil slick and skidded out of control, but when I identified the body the only mark on him was one big hole in his head. No scrapes or bruises."

Brian gently prodded, "How could you tell? The coroner would have only shown you his face."

"I insisted on examining his body at the funeral parlor. You see, the police's explanation sounded fishy to me. Sam always wore a helmet and carried an extra one on the back of his bike in case he picked up some young thing." A brief smile crossed her lips. "The police said there were no helmets at the scene of the accident. I knew it was a lie."

Mrs. Raymonde continued, "I even appealed to the editors of the Headline News to investigate the death of one of their reporter brothers. It was like they had all shut down. I couldn't contact Editor Crawford at all, and Mr Burdon and Ms Menace each gave the same rehearsed answer 'The investigation is closed.'"

A single tear rolled down her pale cheek. She stood in a gesture of dismissal. As she escorted Brian to the steps she asked, "Are you going to investigate further, or are you just doing a follow up story?"

Without waiting for an answer, she closed the door and went inside.

Brian's next stop was at Adam Angler's widow's

townhouse in West Orange. Brian scanned the sheltered layout of the gated community while waiting for the guard to call ahead. Following the guard's brief directions, Brian wended his way through the identical townhouses to find Mai Angler waiting in her doorway.

Mai was of Asian descent with smooth, thick, black hair swept up in a bun. She smiled and opened the door wide for Brian to enter.

Mai sat her petite frame into a large, overstuffed arm chair, and Brian sank into the comfy couch. The entire room emitted tranquility. The thick carpet was a rich, dark sage, offsetting the neutrally tan couch and loveseat. One corner held a small gurgling rock fountain on a tapestry covered table. The room abounded with large hanging plants and tiny bonsai trees. It was quiet. Brian could have lived in that room.

"I understand you want to discuss Adam. We met in Vietnam during the war. Amidst all the fighting and confusion, we miraculously fell in love. Adam managed to bring me to America where we married. I miss him very much." Mai's eyes fell briefly then returned to Brian's.

Brian leaned forward, resting his elbows on his knees. "I want to ask you about his death. I read he was killed in a bar fight. Were you with him at the bar?"

"Oh, no. I do not go to bars. Even if I wanted to, my husband would not permit it. He liked me to stay at home."

"Was his killer brought to justice? There was nothing in the papers about that."

Mai straightened her back and frowned angrily. Her gentle voice reflected backbone for the first time, "They said they couldn't find the man who killed my husband. There were many people in the bar that night, but no one knew his murderer. He ran from the bar and was never seen again. The police said they could not find him.

I tried to talk to Mr Crawford, the editor, but he wasn't available. I finally got through to Ms Menace, but she said she only handled entertainment and gossip, not hard core news."

Mai walked Brian to the door. As she turned back inside, Brian saw a lone tear roll down her cheek.

Over the next two days Brian interviewed any family members he could locate one by one. They each felt the circumstances of their loved ones' deaths were odd, strange, or unusual. Some were sad; some were angry; some were confused, but each one knew something was amiss.

The final interview was of Melinda Menace. Brian had called ahead to explain the reason for his visit. Melinda graciously permitted his interview. Brian pulled his 4 Runner up to a large iron gate leading to Melinda Menace's spacious French Manor home. After identifying himself, the gate swung quietly open and Brian drove the quarter mile to the front of the mansion.

A German maid opened the door and ushered him inside to the library. She offered Brian a brandy, which he declined. He settled into a firm, but comfortable, burgundy wing chair near the huge, stone fireplace.

As he waited impatiently, he perused Menace's book titles. Her books were separated in categories of history, politics, and travel. An entire bookshelf was dedicated to social issues, mostly feminist in nature.

After a fifteen minute wait, Melinda appeared quietly in the doorway. She glided in soundlessly, glancing around as if Brian were not in the room. A moment later Melinda turned to Brian and said, "So, you're here to interview me about the Headline News. This is a switch for me. I'm used to doing the interviewing." She smiled briefly then resumed her reserved demeanor.

Before Brian could speak, she said, "There's not much I'll be able to tell you. I started out as a reporter, much like yourself, and worked up through the ranks until I finally became a Junior Editor. I mostly handled entertainment, gossip, human interest, and the like."

Brian interrupted, "Yes, you have an interesting background, but I really want to know what you know about the dead reporters. Didn't the deaths seem strange to you?"

Melinda leaned back posing her fingers in the teepee position. "I was barely cognizant of their deaths," she replied coolly.

Brian sat up straight and said, "How could that be? These were your co-workers."

Melinda's gaze revealed no emotion. "These reporters worked for Ned Burdon. I had limited contact with them." She uncrossed her legs and leaned forward. "Besides, until you contacted me, I thought their deaths were accidents." She smiled her enigmatic smile again and shrugged.

Brian opened his mouth to pose further questions, but Melinda stood abruptly.

"Unfortunately, I have another appointment. Have a good day Mr Palmer."

In the next moment, Brian found himself standing in the driveway. He drove away satisfied even though he really had gleaned no new information.

Driving down Main Street the evening after the last interview, Brian spied the disheveled form of Malachi Walker shuffling around the corner. Brian cut off a young woman driving a shiny BMW and screeched around the corner to find Malachi. He pulled up along side of him.

Malachi, along with everyone else in the vicinity, had turned toward the screeching sound. He waited patiently as Brian slowed his roll, stopped and opened the passenger side door. Malachi grinned with yellowed teeth, "You don't have to run people over to get to me, Man."

"I guess my nerves are a little frayed." In fact, they were a lot frayed. Brian had taken on the wild eyed look of a trapped animal. He had a two day old scraggly beard, wrinkled clothing and scuffed shoes. He hadn't taken time out for his usual bi-weekly hair cut.

Malachi got in the car, bringing his pungent odor with him. Brian barely noticed. This time they went to another diner on the other side of town. They seated themselves in a back booth.

The waitress gave them a long appraising glance and said, "Which one of you is paying?"

Indignantly, Brian replied, "I am." He pulled out his wallet and slapped a twenty on the table.

Satisfied, the waitress took their orders and strolled into the kitchen.

Malachi laughed out loud, "Whooo wee! You're just getting' a little taste of my life, Man."

Brian grumbled, "Very funny. Now let's get down to business." He related the questionable deaths of the other reporters to Malachi.

Malachi listened intently, but expressed no surprise at the information. He was more interested in his corned beef sandwich and steak fries.

"Are you listening to me?" Brian exclaimed.

"Yeah, yeah, Man." Malachi slurped his hot coffee. "I know all about those other reporters."

Brian sat back in his seat. His eyes registered disbelief. "Why didn't you tell me?"

"If I told you everything in one shot…no more free meals. Right?"

Brian had to admit there was a certain logic to that. "Listen, I think it's too dangerous for you to be on the streets. Maybe you should come home with me…at least until we break the story."

"Oh, now *we're* breaking a story?" Malachi wiped his mouth and said, "And how much are *we* getting paid for this story?"

Brian sighed, "How much do you want?"

"Right now, just enough to get a room for a week."

"But you're coming home with me."

"No, Man. I like my privacy."

Brian offered two twenties. Malachi greedily snatched them out of his extended hand and examined each of them closely. It had been a long time since he held money in his hands.

Brian leaned over the table and whispered, "Malachi, why are you still alive?"

Malachi shrugged his shoulders and answered between swallows of apple pie, "Just lucky, I guess."

Malachi refused to tell Brian where he would be staying, but took Brian's address and telephone numbers with the promise he would contact him if he had any trouble.

Brian arrived home weary, but excited. He entered his foyer, tripped over a fallen book and landed face down amidst piles of papers and overthrown furniture. His home was in shambles. His livingroom had been torn apart. His computer components were disconnected; his books had been pulled from the shelves and thrown to the floor; the contents of his desk drawers had been dumped out. Brian stood stiffly, listening for signs of life. Nothing. He cautiously searched the rest of his house, then called the police.

The police arrived in record time, executed a cursory search of the house, asked the usual questions, wrote a report, and left. Brian didn't offer any possible explanation for the break in. After the information he'd gathered about the dead reporters, he didn't know whom to trust. The cops assumed it was a routine burglary.

Brian spent the rest of the night cleaning up the mess and checking if anything was missing. He started with his desk, his most important area. Besides notebooks he carried in his jacket pocket, all of his notes were on computer disks. He kept them neatly labeled in jewel cases stacked in shoe boxes, a box for each story. The Morning Star box was gone.

His computer cables had been disconnected, and his CPU had been pulled away from his desk. He must have interrupted the theft in progress. Sure enough, he found his back door unlatched. Brian returned and reconnected his computer. He quickly scanned the files be sure his notes were still in his daily journal. Luckily they were.

Now he had proof of what he'd known as soon as he walked in his door. Someone was after him, because of the Headline News story. Bud Light couldn't fix this.

Brian pulled his laptop down from this closet shelf. He only used it on travel assignments, and Burdon wasn't handing any over to him. He copied his Morning Star files onto disks again and packed them carefully; then removed his hard drive from the CPU and packed that.

Brian threw some other essentials into a worn, army green duffle bag, locked his house up tight for all the good it would do, and hopped into his 4 Runner.

Exhausted, Brian bedded down in a hotel on Route 9. He was asleep before his head hit the pillow.

In the morning, over eggs, sausage and coffee in his room, Brian reviewed the previous night's events. If someone was after him, he must be coming close to the real story. He re-examined his notes carefully. His mind held a nagging suspicion that he was missing something important. *What do they always say about investigations? Follow the money. Of course!*

He flipped through his notebook and reread each relative's statement. Each of them was living well on the life insurance money left to them by the deceased reporters. But where is the graft money? These guys made mucho bucks writing for politicians. Some made purchases such as new cars or clothes, but not much surfaced after that. So where was the money?

Brian packed his duffel bag and threw it over his shoulder and set off to find Malachi. As he walked toward the elevator, his mind ran over the places he might look for Malachi. He ducked into the alcove where the Coke and snack machines sat to pick up munchies for the road. As he punched in the keys to get his Snickers Bar, he heard the elevator doors open, then a police radio.

Brian peeked down the hallway to spy two uniformed officers accompanied by a nervous looking concierge.

"Is he dangerous?" The concierge nearly dropped his computerized key card.

The taller officer gruffly responded, "This is routine business. As a matter of fact, just give us the key and wait downstairs."

The concierge handed the policeman the card and scrambled back to the elevator.

Brian watched as the police went to his room and quietly entered. As soon as his room door closed, Brian ran, sans Snickers, to the stairwell. He took the stairs two at a time.

He calmly walked through the busy lobby, passing behind the flustered concierge who was whispering to his colleagues, "They said he might be dangerous. You never know these days."

Brian ducked his head and headed toward his beloved 4-Runner. Halfway across the parking lot he spotted two police officers peering into his car windows with shaded eyes. His car was blocked front and back by a hotel guest's car and a police car.

Brian turned and quick stepped out to the highway.

Luckily he was able to hitch a ride in a black semi driven by a bulky bearded white guy sporting a "Semper Fi" tattoo on his muscular arm.

"Hey, Buddy! Where you headed?" he blurted out in a husky voice.

Brian released a sigh of relief as he threw his bag on the littered floor of the cab and hoisted himself onto the seat.

As they entered bustling downtown Newark, the driver said, "My name's Vinnie. I don't let a lot of people into my cab, but you looked down on your luck."

Brian wiped sweat from his forehead and the back of his neck with the tail of his shirt, then answered, "I'm…," he hesitated. Even though he knew Vinnie couldn't be a cop, he felt the need for caution. "I'm Douglas, and I am a little down on my luck."

"Well, Douggie, things are looking up for you." Vinnie grinned, revealing yellowed, gapped teeth. He reached over and laid a beefy hand on Brian's thigh.

Brian jerked away in surprise, "Hey!"

Vinnie's crooked smile morphed into a snarl. "Did you think you were riding for free?"

Brian grabbed the door handle with one hand and his duffel bag with the other. He pushed the heavy door open and fell into the street just as the light turned green. Horns blared as traffic started moving. Brian scrambled to the sidewalk. He stood, amazed, on the corner of Broad and Market Streets as Vinnie reached over, slammed the truck door, and sped off.

Brian rode a hot, crowded bus back to East Orange. He got off at the stop closest to Leaking Liquors and began his search for Malachi.

Brian caught his quest just as he was leaving the Leaking Liquors parking lot.

Malachi turned to see Brian waving wildly and calling his name. "What's up, Man? You look like crap."

Brian pulled Malachi back into the shadowed lot. "Shut up, Malachi! I need to hang with you for a while."

"With me?" Malachi raised his eyebrows in amusement.

"Yeah, you know, incognito," Brian whispered.

Malachi laughed out loud, "You don't need to be incognito, Man. You already look the part."

Brian stepped into the streetlight to see his shabby, disheveled, dirty appearance. He ran his hand over three weeks of uncut hair and a stubble of five o'clock shadow. He did, indeed, fit the part.

Malachi took Brian to a rooming house on the other side of town. Grunts, sobs, and angry shouts could be heard through the thin walls. The carpet was threadbare, as were the sheets and chenille bedspread. Tattered curtains flapped in the breeze emitting through the dirty, open windows.

Brian looked around and asked, "How can you live like this?"

Malachi just snickered, "You'll see, Man. You'll see."

Brian fell asleep atop the bedspread after drinking a six pack of Bud Light and a pint of Smirnoff vodka. If not for the alcohol, he wouldn't have closed an eyelid. Even as drunk as he was, he couldn't abide the stained sheets.

He and Malachi had stayed up until the wee hours drinking and swapping stories like old war buddies.

Brian needed one night of normalcy, if hiding out in a flophouse could be considered normal. The rules were "no talk about dead reporters or the scandal".

Malachi finally retired to a room down the hall at 3 a.m., leaving Brian to pass out in silence.

At 7 a.m. Brian awoke with a savage urge to pee. After a startled second to remember where he was, Brian sat up, swung his legs over the bedside and kicked his precious duffel bag to ensure it was still there. If he'd been sober, he would have pulled it into bed with him.

He hoisted the bag onto his shoulder and headed down the hall to the john.

Brian quickly washed up, then went to wake Malachi.

Malachi rolled over, licking his chapped lips. "Hey Man, it's early."

"Let's get some breakfast."

At the suggestion of food, Malachi opened his eyes and sat up. "Ok Man. Let's go."

They left Malachi's room just in time to see a seedy, dreadlocked man leaving Brian's room. He was pulling money from a black wallet…Brian's wallet.

"Hey!" Brian yelled. "That's my wallet!" Brian took off down the hall in pursuit weighed down by his duffel bag.

The grimy man dropped the wallet and raced down the back stairs. Brian stopped to pick up his wallet. His cash, driver's license, and credit cards were gone. Brian ran down the back steps, two at a time, to no avail. Mr. Dreadlocks was gone. His stomach turned partially from hunger, partially from fear. Like most citizens, he had no idea how to survive without his credit and debit cards.

Reading his mind, Malachi said, "Come on, Man. I'll feed you." He chuckled and shook his head. "Welcome to my world."

In a few minutes they were standing in front of the Miracle Baptist Church along with fifty other grumbling stomachs. The smell of freshly brewed coffee breezed out to the street.

Brian had never seen such a conglomeration of bags and grocery carts.

Malachi smiled as they inched forward in line, "Man, you're really one of us now."

After a surprisingly filling breakfast, Brian went to a branch of his bank with Malachi in tow.

The guard stopped him at the door. "How can we help you sir?

Brian looked at him quizzically, "I want to take care of some business."

"What exactly, sir?"

Brian frowned angrily, "You didn't stop anyone else."

Malachi chuckled, "I'll wait on the corner."

The guard looked Brian over slowly, then let him in following him with his eyes.

A cautious young woman in a gray business suit and low pumps glanced at the guard before motioning Brian to her desk.

Brian plopped down into his seat and self-consciously brushed off his dusty pants.

The young woman smiled nervously and asked, "How can we help you today?"

Brian explained the theft of his credit cards.

"Do you have I.D. sir?"

"I just explained my license and credit cards were stolen," he sighed in exasperation.

After some back and forth haggling, Brian supplied his social security number and press pass.

After a few keyboard clicks, Ms low pumps went into the back office and reappeared with a tall, slim, stern-looking man wearing horn-rimmed bifocals.

"I'm the branch manager. I must inform you these accounts have been frozen due to a police investigation."

Brian's mouth dropped open.

The manager signaled for the security guard to come over.

The hair stood up on the back of Brian's neck. He leapt from his seat and ran out the back exit into the parking lot. He rounded the side of the building to spy two police cruisers pull up to the bank.

Brian arrived back at the flophouse exhausted and near tears. He sat heavily on the side of the sagging bed and lowered his head into his hands.

He's worked hard to save up a small nest egg which had been his only comfort, besides Bud Light, when Burdon rode his ass.

His pride hedged on the fact that he had pulled himself up from the streets, educated himself with scholarships and part-time jobs, acquired a good position, and built a nice bank account. In a flash, his pride had been stripped from him.

A quiet knock at his door broke into his despair. Malachi appeared calm and smiling. "You ok, Man?"

Brian looked up teary-eyed, "No, Malachi. Do I look alright? Someone's fucking with me, and they're winning."

"You'll be ok, Man. You're with me."

Brian's eyes widened in disbelief. "With you? You live in the streets!"

Malachi replied calmly, "And now, you do too."

No snappy response entered Brian's weary brain. He'd done more than come full circle. He'd dipped below his original circumstances.

Before despondence could overtake him, Malachi spoke, "Don't give up your power, Man."

Brian sneered, "What power? I'm wiped out."

"What about your story, your epic?"

"It's dead. Burdon will never publish it. He's involved."

Malachi grinned, "You don't know that, Man. You don't have one piece of evidence that Burdon has a stake in this."

Brian had to admit he was right. He'd been so focused on Ned Burdon, it never occurred to him his hands could be clean. "But even if he's innocent, he won't publish the story because he hates me."

Malachi sat next to Brian and looked deep into his eyes. "Ned Burdon is a newsman. If your story's good *and* substantiated by solid evidence, he'll publish it. He has to . It's in his blood.

Brian wiped his eyes, stood up, lifted his duffel bag onto his shoulder, and said, "Let's go!"

Back at the Newark Library, Brian clicked the computer keyboard furiously. In three hours he wrote, polished, and documented his story of greed and intrigue. The closing paragraph called for an immediate investigation into the entire affair.

Brian copied the article onto disk and emailed the story directly to Ned Burdon.

Brian went to Malachi who was snoozing peacefully in a chair behind the stacks. Shaking Malachi gently he said, "Let's go, Buddy. It's done."

Malachi grinned, "Let's celebrate. I've got some cash."

Malachi went out and returned in an hour laden with goodies. Beer, chips, sub sandwiches, and cupcakes covered the raggedy bedspread in Brian's room. They feasted like they were dining in the Russian Tea Room in Manhattan. Brian's food had never tasted so good. They talked until the wee hours of the morning.

Brian awoke to being gently shaken by Malachi. He opened his eyes to see Malachi holding up the front page of the Star-Time Press. In two inch letters the headline read "*Political and Press Corruption Exposed*".

Brian sat straight up and snatched the paper from Malachi's hands. He jumped up and did a little happy dance around the room. In a few minutes Brian and Malachi were calling Ned Burdon's direct line from a phone booth.

Brian emerged from the phone booth beaming. He borrowed some bus change from Malachi. "I'll meet you back at my room later."

Malachi waited for the bus to arrive and waved goodbye.

Brian returned to the press room in triumph. The other reporters clapped and cheered as Ned Burdon greeted him like a long lost son. He apologized for the years of harassment.

The Star-Time's exclusive story brought the paper nationwide attention and accolades for having the guts to expose corruption in their own industry.

Burdon escorted Brian into his office and settled behind his desk. Once behind closed doors, his smile dissolved. "Brian, this story is a prize winner. Of course, we've verified the relatives' interviews and news stories of reporter deaths."

"I expected no less," Brian replied confidently. "And thank you for keeping Mr Crawford's name out of this."

"He's the one commonality between us," Burdon replied quietly without looking Brian in the eye. Burdon straightened up in his chair and said, "The only subject we didn't re-interview was Melinda Menace."

Brian looked at Burdon quizzically. "Why not?"

Burdon snorted, "Melinda has a bug up her ass. She had worked hard and pulled herself up through the ranks until she hit what women call the glass ceiling. She was given the title of Junior Editor just like me, but put in charge of fluff pieces, entertainment, fashion, gossip, and stuff like that. She was angry about that. I understood her frustration, but that's the way it was back then." Burdon shrugged. "If I didn't know better, I'd think she'd be a prime candidate to run this whole thing."

Brian and Burdon were each lost in his own thoughts for a moment. As Brian rose to leave he said, "Maybe you better talk to Ms Menace"

"I'll do better than that. I'll make sure she's the focus of the investigation," Burdon said forcefully. "Oh, and we need to meet Malachi Walker in person." Burdon's stern expression implied the urgency of his demand. "You see, the reporter known as Jonas Walker died fifteen years ago."

Brian stuttered, "That's impossible. You're trying to trick me. I'll produce him this afternoon."

Burdon sat back. His jaws relaxed. "Ok, how's three o'clock?"

"Three o'clock it is."

Brian approached the rooming house. *Thank God this is the last time I have to come here.* He bounded up the stairs and knocked on Malachi's door. The door slowly creaked open to reveal an empty room, not that Malachi had any possession to leave there.

A gruff voice from behind startled Brian, "He's gone." The landlord said. He was sweeping the long hallway.

"What do you mean 'gone'?

"He said he was moving on," the heavyset, balding man shrugged. The landlord had no further information and didn't care about anything but sweeping his hallway.

Brian hit all of Malachi's haunts to no avail. As three o'clock quickly approached, Brian became more and more desperate. He went in back of Leaking Liquors four separate times.

At 4:15 p.m. Brian, sweating profusely, arrived at Ned Burdon's office minus Malachi. The other reporters held their collective breaths to hear Burdon's shouts and Brian's pleadings.

Burdon screamed at the top of his lungs, "Not again! You're not going to do to me what you did to Charlie Crawford." He picked up the phone and grumbled "Security? I need you to escort Mr. Palmer off the premises…now!"

Astonished, Brian hung his head and responded, "You don't have to escort me out. I'm leaving."

As Brian stomped out the door, Burdon yelled behind him, "We'll be pressing fraud charges against you!"

Despondent, Brian walked up his old street past his longed-for home only to see an eviction notice pasted conspicuously on the door.

The energy drained from Brian's body and mind. His legs felt like weights. He had no more money for the rooming house, only a couple of bucks to be used for food or Bud Light, whichever he needed more.

He wandered the streets in a daze until he could drag himself no further. When he looked up, he was standing in front of Leaking Liquors. He went inside and bought a single can of Old English 800. *I need to sleep, and this ought to do the job.*

Brian curled up behind the store using his duffel bag as a pillow and pages of his despised Star-Time Press as a blanket.

In the coming weeks Brian watched his house get boarded up, his appearance degrade, and his spirit desert him. He drifted up and down the city streets, ducking into abandoned buildings for shelter and behind restaurants for food.

Brian's beard grew into a stubbly mass with a matching head of hair. His nails were long and dirty. He spent his days rehashing his past deed, regretting his actions. Sometimes he wondered if he imagined the whole scenario.

One chilly night as Fall passed into Winter, Brian lay huddled against the back wall of the Leaking Liquors. He turned on his side to see an envelope with his name neatly printed on the front in block letters. Inside was a postcard showing a picture of a beautiful sandy beach with a deep blue sky and ocean. The back read:

"Thanks for exposing a story which has haunted me for years. I can now rest peacefully. My soul was not calmed by destroying the libelists around me, nor by relieving them of their ill gotten gains. Only the exposure of their sins has relieved me.

"I can live my life out in peace and live well with the money taken from them. Thank you again. Goodbye my friend.

-Malachi"

Brian slumped in the filthy corner, pulled the crumpled pages of the Star-Time Press up to his neck and cried.

Love is like the sea, it's a moving thing; but still it takes its shape from the shore it meets, and it's different with every shore.

Zora Neale Hurston (1903-1960)
Writer

PRETTY YOUNG THING

The first one only cost me a finger. I didn't mean to push him that far, but he wouldn't let go.

It was one of those crisp 1968 autumn afternoons. I had strolled home from work with notions of romantic freedoms dancing in my brain. So many beautiful young men passed me on their way home from the local college campus. I couldn't get them out of my head.

When I arrived home, I told Harry, for the umpteenth time in our six years, our marriage wasn't working. I snatched the soap off the kitchen sink to loosen my wedding band's grip, and tried to get the ring off. I wanted to throw it at him in the dramatic fashion you see in the movies. Instead, in a fury, he grabbed my hand, pulled me toward him, and cut me. It really wasn't that bad. In truth, the loss of a digit was worth it just to get rid of him.

Jesse didn't mind marrying me without my ring finger. He just slipped the gold band on my middle finger and called it a day. He was an eager young man with dreams of buying a house and raising a family. I didn't bother to tell him I didn't want children. After all, children spoil the romance. After a couple of years, this became a bone of contention between us, and the romance died anyway. Who needed such a conventional life? How boring is that?

Jesse's college buddies had tried to dissuade him from marrying me, an older woman. He simply told them our love transcended the ten year age difference. He was poetic that way. That's why I fell in love with him in the first place. But then he spoiled it all, by wanting me to act as a young wife would. You know, one who was starting life anew with dreams of babies and gardening. That just wasn't me.

I don't think he wanted to hack off my arm. He was just trying to stop me from packing. When I saw he meant to stop me from leaving, I tried to run out the door, sans suitcase, but he yanked me back into the apartment. He pulled me into the tiny kitchen and tried to make me sit down. He thought some warm milk would soothe my nerves. I thought *he* should drink some.

I waited for him to turn toward the stove and leapt from my seat. Before I could say, "Boo", he snatched a shiny carving knife from the sink, grabbed my hand, and sliced my arm clean off at the elbow. It was one of those famous Asian knives that you never have to sharpen. I guess they're right. It did the job all right. I was grateful it was my left arm. I use my right one a lot.

The judge let me divorce Jesse right after the trial. He's in the East Jersey State Prison now. Over the years I've just tossed his letters in the shredder. I wouldn't waste time with mail from an old lover. Besides I couldn't chance Rocky seeing them.

Rocky never treated me with sympathy just because I had only one arm. That's why I loved him so. I could tell he genuinely cared about me. It showed in the way he wrapped his arm about me as we walked in the park, and in how he bought me flowers for no reason. We dated for only two months before he proposed the old fashioned way. He dropped down on one knee, presented a beautiful diamond, and simply asked me to marry him. Of course, I said yes. He was a pretty young thing. Well, not much younger, only eight years this time. But at this stage of life, what difference do a few years make?

Rocky was a devoted husband. He did all the right things, worked hard, paid the rent on our luxury high rise apartment, and even cooked sometimes. But he had no passion. I don't mean to say Rocky never made love to me. He did. I just got tired of the standard missionary position once a week like clockwork. Maybe that's why I simply got bored with him. I tried to spice up our love life, but Rocky had his lovemaking down to a science like everything else. He loved the romance more than the physical act. I should have known he was too good to be true.

Rocky tried every way he could think of to dissuade me from leaving. Finally, when he saw I was determined to go, he methodically tied me to the bed and proceeded to saw off my right leg just above the knee with an electric carving knife. He said I wouldn't be able to run from him then. Luckily, he had to pee. When he left the room, I worked off the makeshift gag (he'd tied my own pantyhose around my mouth with the panty part stuffed inside), and screamed my head off.

The doctor said he might have saved my leg if I had gotten to the hospital sooner. I was just grateful he'd saved my life. Rocky jumped from the bedroom window. He's dead. I guess it was all too much for him.

Doctor Ritchie said I could call him Doug (just not in front of other people). He checked on me everyday. As soon as I was fitted with a prosthesis and back home, he dropped by to visit. I thought he was the most thoughtful, generous man I'd ever known. Our wedding bells rang about six months after I arrived home.

We had a year of wedded bliss. Then I began to notice changes. Doug started working a lot of late hours. He had lots more emergency calls than usual. One night I caught a cab to the hospital right after he left our house on one of those calls. I had to see for myself. She was a pretty young nurse in a tight white uniform. She scurried out to Doug's Mercedes and hopped in giggling.

He arrived back home at 6 a.m. Our discussion

was loud and our fight violent. It only cost him his head. He said he couldn't get that young thing out of it. Well, you know how it goes.

"Come to the edge."
"We can't. We're afraid."
"Come to the edge."
"We can't. We will fall!"
"Come to the edge."
And they came.
And he pushed them.
And they flew.

Guillaume Apollinaire,   1880-1918
French Poet, Philosopher

BACKTRACK

"Nooooooooo!" Edress shot straight up in bed. Sweat laced down her face and chest. After a second she realized where she was and switched on the nightstand light. *After all these years, I shouldn't be so shaken.* Her heart pounded.

Only two months had gone by since the last "night panic", as Edress called them. They used to be six to nine months apart, starting when she was seventeen and stalking her into her mid-twenties. If only she could remember them, maybe she could challenge them. But you can't fight what you can't see.

Dr Norman, with his excellent reputation, tried for two years to reach the panic attack roots unsuccessfully. Thousands of dollars later, Edress called the therapy quits to the good doctor's distress. No amount of therapy could help her remember the dreams.

Bringing her knees to her chest, ankles crossed tightly, she wrapped the plaid comforter close to her trembling limbs. Edress rocked gently waiting for her body to stop shaking. She ran her fingers through her matted light brown curls and breathed deeply. It would be hours before she could sleep again. Just in time to arise for work. Isn't that always the way?

"Edress, you look terrible. Are you ill?" Her supervisor peered over reading glasses at the bedraggled girl. "Sit down before you fall down."

Lowering herself slowly before the mound of paperwork, Edress tried once again to fathom the reason for the nightmares. *Yesterday was such a beautiful day. Connie and I went out for lunch and then....*

"Connie, I can't wait for the wedding. What kind of fabric do you want for our bridesmaid gowns? You'll probably get the material free, being Mr Paphian's future niece."

"Great-niece."

Edress quietly added, "Can I wear amber to match my eyes?"

Connie's laughter tossed her black dreadlocks off her shoulders. "No, and your eyes are just light brown. Amber is the color of piss. You can pick out the colors when you get married, if you ever do."

Edress smiled gently and looked at the floor. "If I'm ever lucky enough to meet someone like Bruce, I will."

"Luck has nothing to do with it. You turn down every man who approaches you. When will you learn to trust somebody?"

"I'm not outgoing like you. I can't just approach someone and start talking."

"You should be brave, like when you were in first grade and beat up Butch. Then you kissed him to apologize. You didn't worry about anything back then. What made you change? You're so shy now."

Connie and Bruce were an odd couple. Bruce was the offspring of a Black mother and a White father, taking mostly after Dad. He would often see people staring sidelong at him appraising his racial status. In rebellion he'd dated the darkest girls he could find, until he met Connie. Connie's cocoa skin and black dreadlocks didn't matter as much to him as her wacky sense of humor and beautiful smile. His revolt ended in love.

Bruce's parents loved Connie as a daughter. Watching Bruce and Connie was like seeing themselves 25 years prior.

They floated through aisles of pastel chiffons and rich satins. Paphian's had the best fabric selection in town. It had been here as long as Edress could remember, starting as a small corner store, then expanding to cover one-third the block. Jonas Paphian was bent over, using a cane to get around these days.

"I haven't been in this store since junior high school graduation with Mom. We had picked out this beautiful lemon voile for my dress, then I spilled red wine on it graduation night. I think that's the only time I've ever been in this store. You know Mom is the seamstress in the family."

"She's the seamstress for the whole neighborhood. Has been since we were kids. She's probably here as much as at the grocers'."

Connie selected two lovely shades of fuchsia for the bridesmaid gowns. Old man Paphian rang them up himself, his large hands deftly picking out the register keys. Connie thanked her future great-uncle and sauntered out the door.

A ringing phone brought Edress back to reality. *I just can't understand why this is happening? I refuse to go back to the "couch".* She clicked on her computer and delved into the pile of paperwork.

Sitting up in bed that night, Edress' head drooped, popped up, drooped, popped up over a trashy paperback. She swung her legs over the side of the bed, shuffled to the kitchen and flipped on the coffeepot.

Who can I call at midnight? I need to talk to someone, anyone.

Taking her coffee out to the back porch, she squatted on the stoop and sipped. The hot, black coffee wasn't working fast enough. For two minutes she quick-stepped around the porch. Nothing woke her tired body. Defeated, Edress retired. She blessedly slept through the night.

Connie and Edress passed the next weeks reviewing seating arrangements, flower arrangements and wedding rehearsal dinner arrangements. But the nightmares worsened. Edress arrived at work daily more stressed and worn. Finally on a muggy Saturday morning, Edress jerked awake with one thought...*he's hurting me!*

Leaning on the cluttered dresser, Edress strained her wide, sunken eyes to recognize the sallow-skinned girl drooping in the mirror. Tears streamed down her face in fright. *Who was hurting me?*

Edress gripped the phone with a sweaty palm. Dr Norman's service came on the line. "Dr Norman, is away on business. His office will reopen in two weeks."

"But can't he be reached? Page him. It's an emergency!"

A cool voice responded, "His emergency calls are being taken by Dr Patel at..."

A slammed receiver ended the call. Edress curled up on the bed, shivering in the muggy room until nightfall.

"So what have you been doing, Edie?" Edress' mom put the teapot on the stove. "You haven't been around lately. Are you feeling alright? You look pale." Gloria moved her petite frame across the cheerful kitchen and gently put her palm on Edress' forehead.

"I just had a little virus, Mom, but I'm ok. Connie and I have been working out the arrangements for her wedding. She picked out fuchsia fabric for the gowns. You know Mr Paphian's going to be her great-uncle now. Maybe she can get you a discount."

"He should give me one anyway. I'm in there every other week," Gloria grinned, pushing her gray curls back from her forehead. "I remember you started going there after school for fabric scraps to make doll clothes, shortly after your father passed away."

"What do you mean? I don't remember that."

"Well you sure did. You missed your father so much. I was glad to see you take an interest in something." Gloria paused thoughtfully, "But your spirit never fully returned." Gloria glanced at Edress and frowned. "What's the matter honey? Maybe you shouldn't have come out so soon. You don't look well at all."

Gripping her stomach, Edress lurched up the stairs to the bathroom. She hit the toilet just in time.

That night Edress rolled back and forth in bed, wanting to sleep, not wanting to sleep. She passed out at midnight.

Let me touch you Edie. There's a secret spot that makes little girls happy. Let me show you. A big hand reached toward her skinny thighs. The sickening sweet smell of pipe tobacco smothered her as the hand grew larger and larger....

"Jesus, Edress, what happened to you?" Connie's eyebrows rose to furrow her forehead, as she scrutinized Edress in the morning light.

"The nightmares are back with a vengeance. But something is new. I'm starting to remember things." Edress sat on the edge of the unmade bed in a long sweat-dampened tee shirt and scruffy white socks. "I even tried to get Dr Norman, but he's away."

"Dr Norman? This must be bad," Connie almost whispered. "You said he never helped you. You started the sessions with so much hope. Before each visit you'd say 'Today we'll figure out what's wrong with me. I'm sure of it.' After six months, you were discouraged. In a year, depressed."

"I only stayed another year, because Mom insisted."

"After you ended the therapy, the nightmares stopped. Didn't they?"

"I only had them every once in a blue moon. That really convinced me I made the right decision to stop seeing Dr Norman. Now I wonder..."

"Well, I was going to ask you to come to Paphian's with me, and then go to lunch, but never mind. I can pick this stuff out by myself."

"No, wait. Let me shower. I don't want to fall asleep again."

Twenty minutes later Edress heel-toed it to Paphian's door. She rubbed her rolling stomach, which tightened with each step.

"Do you want to sit in the car? Maybe I should take you to the doctor?"

"No, it's just a virus. It has to pass by itself." Edress shuffled into the air conditioned store, her stomach gurgling. She sat against the first display she reached. Paphian's consisted of two large warehouse-like rooms. One room had clothing fabrics. The other enclosed craft, upholstery and decorative fabrics. Large bins piled with colorful fabrics covered most of the floor space. Low tables butted old file cabinets, which held patterns. Butterick, Vogue and Simplicity pattern books covered the tables. Rows of fabrics on cardboard cores lined the walls. A doorway in the back wall led to Paphian's small office.

Old man Paphian wobbled over smiling, florescent lights glinting off his glasses. "Connie dear, what can I do for you today?"

"Edress' mom said I forgot some of the notions for the bridesmaid gowns."

"Edress?" Paphian turned toward Edress, "Is your mother Gloria McCall?"

"Yes," Edress squinted as the lights reflected off the old man's glasses increasing her headache.

"Your mother's been coming here for years. Gloria's the best seamstress in town. I haven't seen you since you were a little girl. How have you been?"

"Fine."

"Not really," said Connie with a sideways glance at Edress. Connie left Edress to gather the omitted items.

Mr Paphian tilted his head inquisitively, "Why have you stayed away so long?" You used to visit regu-

larly."
      "I didn't even remember coming here until Mom reminded me."
      Paphian smiled, "Oh, so you don't remember." He turned his back to Edress to adjust some merchandise. I guess that's understandable."
      Edress' stomach gurgled. She gripped the display tighter. "Would you please tell Connie I'm waiting outside? I need some air." Paphian looked past Edress. "Wait. Here she comes now."
      Edress met Connie at the register where old man Paphian waited. He stopped to wipe his glasses with a wrinkled handkerchief. As he glanced up, his deep blue eyes looked into Edress' red ones. It was her last memory that day.
      The EMTs gently lifted Edress onto the stretcher. A teary eyed Connie stood stiffly to one side. Edress had clutched her stomach and fainted. She hit the floor before Connie could catch her. Mr Paphian had one of his clerks call 911. The ambulance arrived in minutes.
      The next morning the sunlight streamed through the hospital windows hurting Edress' eyes. She tried to focus. Dr Norman's kind smile slowly came into view. "Connie called me. She said you were trying to reach me. I'm glad to see you, even under these circumstances. So are you ready to begin again?"

      Dr Norman's office was a cool mint green with soft tan chairs and a sink-into-it couch that made you want to stay forever. His desk was a deep mahogany with a brass and wood pen holder, and a green-shaded, brass banker's lamp. The only signs of untidiness were miscellaneous note pads, post-notes and slips of paper scattered over his desk. Seemingly his sole bad habit was excessive note taking.

Dr David Norman was forty-four, graying at the temples and had deep dimples which showed even when he frowned. He moved his tall thin frame through the room quietly so as not to disturb her thoughts.

Dr Norman had considered going into law enforcement, then law, before settling on psychology. He became disillusioned with law when his fourteen year old sister was assaulted. The criminal was released on a technicality. A mere clerical error set the felon free to immediately attack someone else, this time killing the victim. He fled the country and was never found. Why join such an ineffective system? At least in psychology, he could help someone.

Dr Norman's sister was in a deep, long-lasting depression. After years of therapy, she began to recover and was eventually able to lead a normal life. The experience bittered his soul.

Edress perched on the edge of the plush couch, nervously rubbing her hands together. "I'm starting to remember my nightmares," Edress almost whispered. Her eyes darted back and forth as she tried to fathom "why now?".

"What do you remember?" Dr Norman leaned forward in his high back brown leather chair, pen poised.

"Big hands and a smell."

"What smell?"

"Something smothering sweet. Cloying."

"What else?"

"He was saying something, but I don't remember what."

"So it was a man?"

"Yes." Edress tilted her head and squinted trying to surface the memory.

"Now you were in the fabric store when you fainted. Did the fabrics have a smell..."

The session with Dr Norman did not ease her

fears. She knew the nightmare frequency would increase as she got closer to the truth. Edress stayed up past midnight, then couldn't hold her eyes open any longer. Her muscles had relaxed from the pain tablets given her at the hospital, but so had her mind.

Edie, come closer. Give me a hug. You have a sweet little box down there.

Please don't hurt me. I can't breath.

If you tell anyone, I'll hurt your mommy. The next time she comes here I'll get her!

"Nooooooooo!" Edress rolled onto the floor with a thud. "Don't hurt my mommy!"

Edress stretched her arm up and pulled the phone off her nightstand. Dialing frantically Edress tried to quiet her sobs. Her head throbbed as loudly as her heart.

Dr Norman had been laying awake, casebooks and notes spread over his bed. Edress was interesting. In some ways he wished she were not his patient, that they had met in little cafe or the library by chance. But these were just the musings of an older man, wishing for love. After all Edress was young enough to be his daughter. But her smile, her curly brown hair, her frankness and intelligence were the attributes he had been searching for, for years. She was mature and always carried herself as a lady. If he were honest with himself, it was one of the disappointments of her ending the therapy years ago. It was probably the motive behind his giving her his home phone number for emergencies. He smiled. How unprofessional of him. She could be the key to unlock many doors for him. His phone jangled him out of his reverie.

Edress dashed to the door before the ding donged. She smelled softly sweet from the fruity shower gel she used right after she called him. A feeling of safety entered the house with Dr Norman.

Dr Norman surveyed the disheveled room as he

settled into a soft, pastel print armchair. Edress settled onto the peach-colored couch across from him. The small coffee table between them held half-melted scented candles in wrought-iron and green glass holders and a couple of literary magazines, all covered with a thin layer of dust. Edress stared desperately into his eyes.

"He said he'd hurt my mother if I told anyone what he was doing to me." Edress paused, then whimpered, "He was molesting me." A small squeal escaped her throat, and the tears rolled down her cheeks.

Instantly Dr Norman was at her side. She sobbed into her sanctuary. Hours of weeping melted into heavy slumber. David Norman held his patient until morning.

That afternoon Edress settled back into Dr Norman's couch. Her first good sleep in eons had put color back into her cheeks. Dr Norman sank into his large leather chair and fumbled inside his tweed jacket for a pen. He wet his thumb and flipped to a clean page on his steno pad.

"OK, Edress, can you remember anything else about the dreams? I know they fade fast, but anything would help." Dr Norman kept his eyes on his pad. But, oh, her eyes had a mischievous little flash.

"No, nothing."

"I'd like to try hypnosis. Now that the details are coming forward, hypnosis should be able to bring them to the surface."

Edress stiffened and rose to a sitting position. "I don't want to regress there. I'm afraid to bring back the memories."

Dr Norman arose and gently pushed Edress back onto the couch. "You'll be safe. It will seem like a dream."

"You mean nightmare."

"I'll be right here. You'll be able to hear my voice

the entire time. I'll bring you back at the first sign of distress."

Edress paused then asserted, "No, if I'm going to do this, I'm going all the way."

Dr Norman closed the blinds and dimmed the lights. He spoke slowly and smoothly. "Now just relax. Close your eyes. Listen to my voice…"

The transition took three minutes. Edress proved to be pliable despite her prior resistance. Edress reposed, slumber-like on the soft couch. One arm lay at her side, the other across her lap. Her head was propped up on two throw pillows.

"Go back, Edress, to the first time your molester approached you. How old are you?"

"I'm eleven. I want some fabric scraps to make doll clothes."

In even tones Dr Norman asked questions. "Where are you?"

"I'm with him," Edress answered in a soft, tiny voice.

"What do you see around you?"

"A big desk and a chair with wheels. He's reaching for me. His hands are so big!" Edress raised her hands defensively.

"You're safe Edress. I'm here." Edress relaxed slightly, lowering her hands. "Can you see his face?" Dr Norman's concentration drew him forward.

"I see thick smoke. He has a pipe. The smell is sweet, sickening. He's leaning over me," Edress squealed like a scared puppy. "Don't hurt me!"

Dr Norman struggled to control his voice, "It's OK Edress. This is just a dream"

"He's swept his arm across the desk. Swatches of fabric are floating to the floor. He wants me to sit on the desk," Edress' voice crescendoed. "No, don't touch me!"

"Can you see his face? Who is he? Who is he?"

Dr Norman's voice tensed despite his efforts. "No, Mr Paphian! Nooooooooo!" Edress screamed and fainted.

A few minutes had passed since the nightmarish session. Handing Edress a glass of water, Dr Norman asked, "How do you feel now."

"I don't understand why I blocked it out all these years." Edress steadied the glass with both hands. Her wide eyes stared at nothing. Her body quivered. "How could he have done this to me?"

"He's a sick person. My concern is what are you going to do?"

"I'm going to press charges! I'm going to get him!"

"Now wait a minute. This happened almost 15 years ago."

"Whose side are you on? Don't you believe me?"

Stern words did not disguise the tender concern in his eyes. "Of course I believe you, but that won't be enough. You'll need proof."

That night Edress sat curled up on her livingroom couch. The brrriiiiiiiing of the telephone jolted her out of her reflections. "Hi Connie."

"What's wrong? You sound strange."

"Nothing. I was asleep." How could she tell Connie about her soon-to-be great-uncle?

"C'mon girl. You've always told me everything. I know something's wrong. If you don't tell me now, you'll tell me later," Connie teased.

Edress sat mutely.

Connie retorted to the silence, "Well, I just wanted go over the rehearsal dinner plans with you. Let's get together over breakfast. OK?"

Edress tried to keep her voice light. "Let's make it lunch. I have something to do in the morning."

The next morning Edress, armored with prayer and coffee, drove to Paphian's. She parked in front of the diner across the street and looked around. Other than the few store owners opening their shops, the sidewalks were deserted. Gathering her strength, she marched right up to Paphian's back as he unlocked the iron gates covering his entryway. Without turning Paphian murmured, "I knew you'd come."

He turned to face Edress. His smirk sickened her.

"You *do* remember."

"I'm old, not senile." The smirk widened.

"How could you have hurt me? I was just a little girl."

"Isn't that when it happens to everyone? Are you back for more? You're too old now. I like them young."

Edress listened, mouth agape.

"Besides, you wouldn't like it now. I had to give up my pipe. Doctor's orders, you know. You loved the smell. That's how I got you into my office ...the first time," Paphian cackled.

Edress swallowed back angry tears. "I'm going to put you away! I'm going to the police!"

"Who's going to believe you? I'm a longtime businessman in this community. Your own mother shops here."

"Don't you ever mention my mother again!" Vomit rose in Edress' throat.

"Why? She won't believe you either. You obviously never told her."

"She doesn't need to know. She's an old woman now."

"Your own guilt keeps you from telling her, and what about Connie? Are you going to ruin her wedding? Pull her away from my family? I'd be heartbroken," sarcasm spat from his grin.

Edress spun and ran toward her car. Hot tears flew off her cheeks. Her breath hitched. She jumped into her Toyota and sped off with no destination in mind. Her thoughts raced. *He's right. How can I prove it?*

Edress' sick stomach erupted all over her clothes as she put her key in her front door. After mopping the porch, she showered, donned her yellow silk robe, and headed for the kitchen.

Edress made a cup of Chamomile Tea. She was just steadying the mug to her lips when the phone rang. She whispered, "Yes?"

A voice crackled, "Hi Edie"

The mug crashed to the tiled floor. Steamy liquid splashed her bare legs. "What do you want Mr Paphian?"

"You still show respect. Your mother taught you well."

"What do you want?"

"I was just wondering why the police haven't ar- rive yet."

"You son-of-a…"

"But I'm patient. I can wait for a lot of things… except one thing."

"What?"

"I can't wait until Connie and Bruce have a little girl. You know, someone I can play with?"

Edress' blood turned to ice water. She slammed the receiver down and fled to her bedroom, leaving behind a puddle of broken glass and tea.

That afternoon in a bustling café, Connie chattered over her burger and salad, "I'm glad you made it. There's so much to go over."

Edress barely heard her. "Connie, I need to talk to you."

"When will you surprise me with the shower? I want to look good that day."

"The shower?" Edress had totally forgotten.
"...and the bouquets will be white roses with fuchsia ribbons..."

"Connie, please!"

"What? The wedding is two weeks away! We still have details to handle."

"Connie, I have something important to say." With a pained look, Edress plunged ahead, "I just found out I was molested as a child."

Connie inhaled, fork frozen mid-air.

Edress explained the whole story.

Connie's eyes widened, then narrowed. "Are you trying to spoil everything? This is Bruce's family! Why are you saying these things? Because I'm getting married and you're not? No wonder you're not excited for me. I bet you haven't even planned a shower!"

People turned and stared.

"Do you think I'm lying to you? If Bruce loves you, this won't matter to him."

"I thought you loved me too. I can't believe you would do this to me!"

Connie jumped up, slammed money on the table, and stomped out. A stunned Edress sat tearfully holding her cramped stomach.

That night as Edress sat on her bed yoga-style, back against pillows, the phone rang. She answered hopefully, "Connie?"

A voice whispered, *You little slut. No one will believe you.*

Edress gasped and dropped the receiver. Low laughter emitted from the comforter. She swiped the phone off the bed. It crashed to the carpet. The dial tone hummed. The phone lay there until morning.

The doorbell awakened Edress at 8a.m. She inched out of bed, rubbing the back of her aching neck. Except for shoes, she was still fully dressed. Creeping to the front door, she picked up an iron candleholder from the hall table. She held her makeshift weapon high and peeked out the peephole. There stood Connie looking around with sad puppy eyes. Edress let her in with relief. "Edress, I'm sorry. I was so selfish. You were right. I told Bruce last night. He sympathizes, but of course, he can't go against his family."

"Why not?"

"Bruce told me his uncle suffered from depression as a kid. He thinks something bad happened to him in his childhood, but his family won't disclose details." A silent moment of awareness passed between them. Connie looked down at her shoes and quietly added, "I wish I didn't know anything about this. I was so happy." A single tear rolled down her chocolate cheek. Their hug lasted for five minutes. Connie was soon on her way, leaving a much-consoled Edress.

Edress sat silently, deep in thought, the wrought iron candlestick at her feet. She almost pitied Paphian... almost.

Encouraged by Connie's sympathy, Edress showered and dressed quickly. After checking all her window and door locks, she walked to the driveway and climbed into her Toyota. She pulled forward. *Crrrrunch! Now what?* Edress got out and rounded the car to find a flattened spray can under her front passenger tire. She bent to pick it up, then froze. Huge black letters sprawled across the side of her car, "SLUT".

Endless minutes passed before Edress stood up and looked around. There was no one in sight.

Edress took a taxi to Dr Norman's office. He was waiting at the door. Ushering her inside, Dr Norman said, "Edress, you're in danger. I want you to go to the police."

"What are they going to do? Write out a vandalism complaint? I didn't see anyone in the area this morning except Connie. I don't even know when it happened."

"Would Connie do this?"

"Connie loves me!" But inside she wondered.

"I know someone who might help you, but I'd have to reveal your situation. Do you trust me?"

"Yes Doctor."

"You should be calling me David by now. We've gotten too close for formalities." His arms were a protective blanket around Edress' shoulders.

Edress nearly collapsed with relief and let the tears flow. "Thank you David." A long-denied well of emptiness and fear was filled with comfort and warmth. She looked up into his eyes, awaiting the inevitable kiss. He bent and kissed her forehead, her eyelids, her throat and finally her waiting lips.

That afternoon the doorbell chimed jarringly. Cautiously, Edress inched to her door and peered out to find a pale young woman with stringy, shoulder length, blonde hair. "Who is it?"

Blondie jumped and answered softly, "Dr Norman sent me. I'm Sarah LeMonde."

Edress opened the door, looked up and down the street, then let her in.

Sarah stood nervously in the dim light of the foyer, wringing her hands. She wore an unflattering, long, loose, pastel, flowered dress and white loafers.

Edress relaxed. "Why are you here?"

"I'm here to help you."

Edress muffled a titter at the thought this shaken creature could aid her.

Sarah sat her thin frame on the sofa and tugged softly at an unadorned ear. In fact, she wore no jewelry of any kind. Edress perched across from her on the arm of her fat leather chair. Sarah began, "I just wanted you to know you're not alone. He molested me too. I was only ten years old. I've been in therapy on and off ever since. I used to pass Paphian's on my way home from school

school. The fabric colors fascinated me. I'd just stop and stare in the windows. One day Mr Paphian came out and asked if I wanted to feel the different fabrics. I stopped by every day after that. He always made time for me." Sarah hesitated, breathed deeply, then proceeded, "One day he said he had some special fabrics in his office. I followed him in. His office smelled of cherry pipe tobacco. Fabric swatches lay on his desk. He picked me up and sat me on his desk…for a closer look." Tears welled up in Sarah's eyes. "My life changed forever that day."

Edress looked silently at the floor. The words took a few seconds to sink in. Edress jumped to her feet with joy. "Thank God! Finally a witness! We can go to the police together. They'll have to believe me now."

Sarah's eyes widened. "No, I can't discuss this in public. I'm not ready for people to know what happened. Dr Norman said I would only have to talk to you."

"How can you live without revenge?"

"My revenge is helping other victims. I'm a nurse at County General. I have treated countless victims of incest, rape and abuse. They come into the hospital every-day. Between counseling others and going to therapy, I'm living well."

"You're just existing. Don't you see, convicting him would be the best therapy for both of us? Don't you want to feel safe again? I know I do." Edress looked pleadingly into Sarah's eyes.

"He's an old man; he can't hurt me anymore."

Connie snapped, "He hurts us everyday he's free. Don't you want justice?"

"Yes. I hope you can get it for us."

She left as silently as she had appeared.

That night Edress slept fitfully, fully dressed on top of her comforter. She had fallen asleep crying in dis-appointment and fear, feeling more alone than ever. Sud-denly she bolted upright. What was that sound? Something bumped against the front door. Crawling out of bed, Edress slinked along the floor on hands and knees to the hallway. Moving only her head, she followed the sound of rustling bushes along the side of the house. Someone was moving to the back door. The back stoop creaked.

Edress leapt up and raced to the front of the house. She tore open the locks, ran out the front door, and tripped falling hard to her hands and knees on the wooden steps. She looked back over her shoulder to see a battered black cardboard shoebox beneath her ankles. Pushing up painfully, she stood, than stooped to pick up the box. A worn rubber band held the lid securely. She slid off the band and without breathing, slowly removed the top. Edress took one look and thought she'd never breathe again. Her world began to gray out. Edress fell back into her foyer before blacking out totally.

Edress awakened in the dark, sprawled on her back on the hardwood floor. The front door was ajar, allowing a chilly breeze to run over her body. Everything ached. She slowly rolled over and painfully stood up. She flicked on the hall light to reveal the shoebox contents spilled out on the floor… a tawny-haired rag doll with lace panties pulled down around her ankles.

Edress stood shaking for a minute, then took a deep breath and calmed to a cool stillness. She picked up the phone and called David. His machine answered efficiently, then beeped. Edress' voice mirrored the answering machine's coldness, "I'm putting this to an end now."

Fifteen minutes later Dr Norman emerged from a steamy shower. Rubbing his strong back with the rough terrycloth towel, he strolled to his bed. Throwing the towel onto his nightstand, he stretched out on the bed, hands behind his head, the blinking message light on his answering machine unseen through the towel.

Edress quickly dressed all in black. Nike running

shoes, stretch pants, pullover long-sleeved top, baseball cap. She rolled up a three-yard length of sackcloth retrieved from her mom's fabric stash, hopped in her rented Volkswagen and drove off hurriedly.

The next morning Edress sat huddled behind a newspaper in the diner across from Paphian's store. Paphian's mouth dropped open when he saw the huge crudely printed cloth sign hung across the storefront, "PEDOPHILES ON SALE". He spun around, eyes searching the street for signs of life. Then he quickly yanked the sign down and took it inside. He slammed the door behind him, turned, peeped out, and disappeared into the dark store.

Edress hit the message button on her answering machine upon her return home. "You think you're so smart," Paphian croaked. "I know it was you. Don't try to play my game."

A shiver of triumph coursed through Edress.

That afternoon Edress pulled up in front of Gloria's house. David had had her Toyota repainted. It looked brand new. Edress walked up the lane, noting the overgrown hedges. On her mother's worn, flowered welcome mat was a plain white envelope. The words "LOOK INSIDE" were scrawled across the front in the same crude penmanship used to vandalize her car. Edress snatched the envelope up and ripped off the short edge. She yanked the folded sheet out and opened it. The letters and words cut out of magazines spelled, "YOUR DAUGHTER IS A WHORE".

The door clicked open. Edress shoved the envelope into her pocketbook. Gloria asked, "Why didn't you ring the bell? If I didn't happen to look out the window, I wouldn't have known you were here." Then with a concerned look, "What's the matter baby?"

"Nothing, Mom. Has anyone been here today?"

"No, and you haven't been around either. I thought you said you were feeling better? You don't look well."

In the kitchen, Edress choked down a slice of chocolate cake and cup of tea while Gloria prattled on. "I stopped in Paphian's today for some lace. You know he can barely get around anymore. He has to use a cane just to cross the room."

Edress stopped mid-bite. "Mom, I have to run an errand. I'll talk to you later." She sped to David's office.

"David, how could he get the doll to my house or leave this envelope at Mom's? He hobbles."

"Someone's helping him, but whom? You've only confided in Connie and me. Didn't Connie come by the day your car was vandalized?"

"She wouldn't hurt me." Outwardly Edress was steadfast. Inside she wondered.

"By the way, what did you mean in your phone message? You're not thinking of doing anything dangerous are you? I don't want you anywhere near that man. He might hurt you."

"I'm not afraid anymore, David."

David tensed, "Stay away from him. Do you understand?"

"This is my battle, David. Either you're with me or against me!"

David sighed resignedly, then pulled her close. He whispered in her ear, "I'm with you."

That evening Connie arrived at Edress' door and tearfully announced, "The wedding's off."

"What happened?"

"Bruce was kidding me about having tin cans tied to the bumper of our limo as a joke. Then he said it would be better than having "slut" painted on the side."

Edress gasped.

"He tried to catch himself, but couldn't. You

should have seen the horrified look on his face when he realized what he said. You had just told me about the vandalism a couple of hours before he mentioned it. I never told anyone."

"So you broke off the engagement?"

"I threatened to go to the police. He called me a traitor and broke the engagement." Connie melted into tears again.

"We've got to turn him in immediately!"

"He's gone."

"Gone where?"

"I went to his apartment to talk to him. It was emptied out. His suitcases and clothes were gone. He only left the wedding tux." Connie burst into heavy sobs. It was Edress' turn to console someone.

Leaving David's office after filling him in on the details, Edress crossed the street to her shiny Toyota. The streetlights glinted off the new paint job. She winced at the memory of the covered unpleasantness. Suddenly Edress jumped at the sound of screeching tires. She turned just in time to see a large dark car bearing down on her. At the last second she leapt, belly first, onto the hood of her beloved Tercel. The careening vehicle smashed the driver's side door flinging Edress over the hood, slamming her to the sidewalk.

David raced across the street yelling, "Edress! Edress, are you alright? Somebody dial 911!"

Edress awoke in a sanitized County General room. David's face swam into view. "What happened?" Edress whispered. She tried to rise, but her aching muscles protested.

"A car almost ran you over. You're ok though. You have a sprained ankle and a few contusions. You just have to stay overnight. I arranged for this private room."

A policeman arose from the corner chair. Edress

had not noticed him before. He stepped over to the bed and pulled a pad and pen from his uniform belt. "Ma'am, are you up to a few questions? We need to know what happened."

"A car came out of the dark. His lights weren't

you get a look at the driver?"

ut I know who it was." She explained the

he officer.

ı prove any of this?"

ɔke up. "I know it was him. Who else

told me earlier you only saw the rear of

tance in the dark. You weren't even out-

ened."

"But I can corroborate Miss McCall's story up un- til that point."

The officer lowered his pad and looked David in the eye. "What exactly if your relationship with Miss McCall?"

David murmured downheartedly, "She's my pa- tient, I mean, my girlfriend."

The officer smirked smugly, "I'll be in touch with both of you." He strode out of the room, leaving a film of insecurity behind.

David sat on the edge of the bed, "I'm sorry, Hon. I want to force them to believe you're in danger."

"You can't make them believe without proof. You told me so yourself."

"I'll find a way."

"David, I have faith in you. We can do this to- gether." Edress' eyes closed as the medicine reclaimed her. "I have to sleep now. Please don't leave me alone."

"I just have to go home to get my pager and toothbrush."

But Edress was already sound asleep.

Edress lay sleeping in the quiet hospital coolness. Her swathed swollen ankle lay elevated upon a fat pillow. The florescent lighting from the hall blanketed her room with a dim glow. The large wooden door swung shut with a quiet click and blackened the room. Edress slowly opened her eyes, "David, is that you?"

Suddenly smothering softness covered Edress' face. *Am I dreaming? No!* She clawed at the pillow which held her breath in her throat. Her mind screamed silently. She struggled freeing her legs from the tightly tucked sheets. Her drug-induced weakness left her helpless against this overpowering force. She fought in slow motion, dream-like. Edress slowly weakened. Her limbs went limp. A scream from the doorway spearheaded the pillow's release. Air flooded her throat and nostrils. Edress rolled off the bed and passed out on the cold tile floor.

She re-awakened to a flurry of activity and bright lights. David was once more by her side. A doctor and two nurses fussed over her, checking her vitals.

As the hospital staff left, a plain clothes policeman entered the room. "Miss McCall, can you tell me what happened?" Tall, pale, disheveled and tired-looking, he pulled a small pad from inside his wrinkled sport coat.

"Not really. I thought I was dreaming. Then I realized someone was trying to smother me. I tried to push him off. The next thing I remember is waking up a few minutes ago."

"Did you see the assailant?"

"Here we go again," Edress sighed.

"What does that mean?

"Oh nothing." She looked longingly at David, wishing to escape to a faraway peaceful island with him.

"You were lucky that nurse interrupted the guy, or you might not be alive. She's giving our other detectives a description now."

A few minutes later Edress and David were alone again. "Why did you leave me David?"

"I had to bet my beeper. When I got back, the police were here."

"Don't leave me again," Edress slurred. Her eyelids drooped.

"It's ok to sleep now Edress. I'm staying all night." David held her cold hand in his warm ones long after she fell into a deep sleep.

The next morning Edress ate her breakfast ravenously. David sipped coffee retrieved from the cafeteria. The detective from the previous evening entered frowning.

"Miss McCall, I just wanted to know if you've remembered any other details from last night."

"No, I'm sorry."

"If you remember anything, please call me. As of now we have little to go on. We only had one witness, and she gave a very general description. She was too frightened to be much help." He turned to leave.

"Detective, wait. I would like to thank the nurse who saved me."

"I'm afraid that won't be possible. Nurse LeMonde's gone."

Both David and Edress jerked to alertness.

David's voice rose, "What do you mean 'gone'? Maybe she's been hurt or worse!"

"We made a follow up call to her home this morning. She moved out. Her belongings were gone. She left no forwarding address. We needed her as a witness. She must have gotten scared. If we find her, I'll be sure to let you know." He left without saying goodbye.

"Nurse LeMonde?" Edress wrinkled her forehead. "Why is that name familiar?"

David leaned nearer, "It must have been Sarah. The girl I sent to you last week. Remember?"

Edress' eyes filled with awareness. "She had to be

coming to see me. I forgot she worked here."

"She must have been scared senseless. It was the first time she confronted her molester." Concern covered David's face.

"We should tell the police about her connection to Paphian."

"We can't betray her trust. She doesn't want anyone to know about her past."

"Even to save her life?"

"The detective said she moved. Would a murderer bother to pack her things? Be logical. I'm sure she ran away."

Edress acquiesced, "Well, she was pretty timid." Then smiling, "Downright shaky as a matter of fact."

They laughed lightly, then heartily. Tension rolled off their shaking shoulders.

That afternoon after the doctor's final examination, David brought his sweetheart to his home. "Don't walk so fast. You're still healing."

"I'm just glad to be out of the hospital. Besides it doesn't hurt much." Edress did a quick limp over the cobblestone path to his hunter green front door.

Once inside, David made her comfortable on his king-sized bed, propped her leg onto a pillow, and put the phone and TV remote by her side. "Is there anything else you'll need until I get back?"

Edress settled deep into the fluffy pillows piled behind her back, "Just return quickly." She glanced around at the peaceful blue and green hues encompassing the bedroom.

"Don't worry. I will. Besides no one knows you're here. You'll be safe until I get back from your place."

"Remember to bring my chamomile tea and fuzzy slippers." Edress giggled contentedly.

As soon as David shut the front door behind him,

Edress hopped off the bed and began to poke around. His home mimicked his neat office. Each room was carpeted in muted earth tones with matching print curtains. A large fish tank gurgled softly from one corner of the livingroom. A large stone fireplace graced one wall. Soft, ethnic-print throw pillows adorned the low black leather couch. Down the hall the bathroom porcelain sparkled. The modern kitchen was immaculate, making Edress a little ashamed of her own.

A closed door clicked open into a darkened room. Edress fumbled for the light switch and flipped it on to reveal a den. Orderly bookshelves lined the walls on either side. Edress inched along one wall and studied the titles. The books ranged from detective novels to law enforcement texts to psychology books. A lounge chair and small table with a reading lamp comfortably filled one corner. Edress felt, before she saw, something was amiss here. She glanced across the room to see a chaotic mess. David's desk was a shock of papers piled high. Her ankle started to ache. She limped to the messy scene. Papers cluttered the large desk and were scattered on the surrounding carpet like dead Autumn leaves. She sifted through them curiously. The papers looked like drafts of letters and reminder notes. Some of the letters were written two and three times with multiple scratch-outs and errors. She lifted one to read it through.

"I rewrite my letters until I get them right!"

Edress almost fell over at David's booming voice. She turned to see him standing in the doorway, arms crossed, eyebrows raised, smiling.

David helped Edress to a chair in the livingroom. His demeanor turned serious.

"Your place was broken into, while you were in the hospital. There were scratch marks in the door frame, like the lock was jimmied."

"Was my place wrecked?" Edress' eyes teared.

"No and I didn't see anything out of place. You should notify the police and change your locks immediately."

"That's not going to do any good. Why go through the exercise?"

They sat silently a while. Then David went into the kitchen and brewed the chamomile tea.

After a short nap, Edress call home to check her messages. One beep. Holding her breath, Edress waited for the message. The phone filled with creepy laughter. She forcefully slammed the receiver, cracking it. Then she picked it up and dialed.

Saturday morning Edress sat in David's cheerful breakfast nook rapidly flipping through the morning paper.

"Looking for a sale?" David grinned and poured orange juice into two large glasses.

"As a matter of fact I am."

"Well I guess you're fit enough to go shopping. The change might do you some good."

"I'm not going to buy anything, but I might stop by to look." She triumphantly flipped open to a full page ad.

PAPHIAN'S GOING OUT BUSINESS SALE!
75% OFF ALL FABRICS AND NOTIONS

David cocked his head and frowned. "Paphian's going out of business?"

"Let's go!" Edress insisted.

They parked across the street from Paphian's in the diner's lot just in time to see the police arrive. A large, angry, mostly female, mob was trying to push past Paphian into the store. Paphian was waving his arms wildly, yelling for them to get back. He kept trying to close the door but the raging throng kept moving forward. Edress giggled uncontrollably until tears ran down her cheeks. David divided his gaze between the riot at Paphian's and Edress' red face.

"Edress, did you have something to do with this?" He looked at her suspiciously.

Between little gulps of air, Edress answered, "I placed the ad in the paper. I pretended I was Paphian's assistant and called it into the newspaper. It was easy. I just told them to put it on the account." Edress dissolved into guffaws, holding her stomach. "Now close your mouth and drive me to the rear of his store."

"Will you help me or not?" Edress gazed into his eyes. David could not resist.

They drove to the rear of Paphian's. Edress slipped into the rear door used only as an office entrance. She could hear the cacophony at the front of the store. In five minutes she returned to the car. They drove away unnoticed.

David tilted his head inquisitively, "Well, what did you do?"

"I just wanted to get a closer look."

Unbelieving, David remained silent.

It was a beautiful evening. The cool breeze offset the warm air perfectly. David and Edress drove out to the Brimley restaurant. The restaurant was on a large boat docked at the pier. They stopped on the dock before entering. Edress held the single red rose David had given her when she had entered the car. David wrapped his arm around her shoulders as they looked over the water. The moment was perfect peace.

After a candlelit dinner of champagne, lobster, asparagus tips and chocolate mousse, they drove to David's house in quiet anticipation.

Entering the foyer, David swept Edress into his arms and kissed her fervently. Edress dropped her rose and handbag on the carpet. He swooped her up and carried her upstairs to his king-sized bed. Edress caught her breath. He lay her down gently and stretched out beside her. Only the moonlight revealed their movements. Again they kissed. David moved his lips to her neck, causing Edress to roll her head gently in the downy comforter. A slight moan escaped her throat. Slowly David unbuttoned the front of Edress' peach silk blouse revealing her breasts bursting over her pink lace bra. He kissed the soft mounds. Then traced tiny kisses down to her navel. There he lingered, causing Edress' stomach to rise from the bed. She ran her fingers over his hair, pushing his lips deeper into her flesh. David sat up and pulled off his soft wool sweater to reveal a smooth, dark, muscular chest. Edress lay dreamlike as his body captured her senses. He abandoned his sweater, lifted her shoulders from the bed and pulled off her blouse. Reaching behind her, he pulled off her bra in one swift movement. Edress lay back and raised her hips to pull off her skirt. David obliged her, almost ripping it in his heat. He threw down his pants, revealing his passion. For one tense moment, David stood and allowed his eyes to feast on her supple body dressed only in pink lace panties. Then he plunged onto her nakedness. His hot lips sought Edress' nipples hungrily. Her hands explored every muscle from his thick shoulders to his rippling buttocks. David slid his hot body downward and kissed the lace edges of Edress' panties. She moaned loudly and raised her hips to meet his kisses. He wrapped his strong arms around her hips and squeezed savagely, burying his face in the crevice between her thighs. Edress screamed, wanting to let him in, but he wrapped her legs even tighter making her beg for relief. David released his grip and lay his face in the moistness between her thighs. Slowly, tortuously, he kissed and nipped Edress around the edges of her panties, lifting her legs to cover her buttocks with little love bites.

Edress could stand no more. She wrapped her legs around David's neck and moaned, "Take me." David reached underneath her, pulled her panties off, and mounted her like a black stallion. He crushed her breasts with each thrust. The bed rocked and rumbled. Their bodies battled as if to beat back the tensions of past weeks. Suddenly David stiffened and arched his back. He grimaced as if in pain. He and Edress simultaneously screamed their pleasure and sighed blessed release. They slept in each other's embrace.

Early Sunday morning while he slept soundly, Edress stole David's car keys. She loaded two large, bulky, black garbage bags into his trunk and drove to Paphian's rear door. All was quiet. No one moved in the back alley leading to Paphian's office. The back windows were sealed with wired gates, which had long since rusted solid into the cement wall. High above the windows was an old one and a half foot square slotted vent. Rust over moldy green paint gave it an antique verdigris look. A five-foot wide weathered garbage bin on dented rubber wheels stood near the corner of the store.

Edress laboriously pushed the empty garbage bin until it was underneath the vent. Then she climbed on gingerly favoring her newly healed ankle. She reached up, grabbed the vent and pulled herself upright. Using a screwdriver Edress took turns at each vent corner, tediously loosening it from the wall. Finally with a tug, the vent screeched free and dropped to the ground.

After retrieving the garbage bags from the trunk, Edress squeezed them, one by one, through the vent. They plunked softly to the office floor. Then, entering legs first, she lowered herself into the room. At last hanging, arms outstretched, Edress dropped the final three feet to a painful landing.

The office was dimly lit from the alley windows. All was quiet. Edress quickly went to work. Fifteen minutes later she walked out the back door setting off a silent alarm. She was back in David's kitchen before the excitement began. David had not stirred.

Later that morning David returned to his apartment with the Sunday paper and exciting news. "Paphian's had a fire. Someone broke in, and set wastebaskets filled with pipe tobacco on fire all around the store. The smoke set off the sprinklers. Either smoke or water ruined all of his fabrics. Paphian broke down and cried. He loves that store. It's his life."

Edress listened intently to every detail, but said nothing. Even though she trusted David, she couldn't involve him in her crime.

Monday's paper carried the story describing the tobacco stench and soggy ruined fabrics. There was a photo of Paphian leaning against his building, face in hands, weeping. He had come under suspicion of arson and fraud, and had to be hospitalized from the strain. His insurance company refused to pay for damages unless he was cleared of all charges.

Paphian lay exhausted in his private hospital room. No flowers, cards or visitors had passed through his door. His dinner tray lay untouched. The slightly opened blinds allowed gray slits of the setting sun to ride over his thin, motionless frame. A sedative flowed through him intravenously. A dim light from the quiet hallway glowed over him turning his face into a death mask. Edress stood watching Paphian a long time before creeping in and shutting the door. He no longer looked like the menacing ogre of her night panics. She almost pitied him…almost. She leaned over his prone body and shook him.

Paphian awoke with a start. Edress clapped a hand over his mouth. "Quiet," she whispered.

Paphian nodded his submission. Edress removed

her hand. "I'm here to give you a last chance to confess."

"Why should I? What else can you take from me? My business is ruined. That was my life. My brother blames me for Bruce's disappearance."

"How about your reputation? You cherish that too. People will forget arson and fraud charges, especially if they're dropped, but they'll never forget child molestation, even if I can't prove it."

"What difference does it make if you charge me or if I confess? Either way I'd be ruined."

"I'll go to the newspapers, TV, radio, whoever will listen. These people will lynch you. Every girl you've molested will come forward once the news is out. If you confess, you can give yourself up to the police quietly."

"My molester never confessed."

Edress froze.

Paphian continued dreamlike, "I was my uncle's favorite nephew. He'd take me fishing. Just me. My brother was so jealous. Uncle Steven said we were buddies. We kept secrets between us." Paphian's eyes rolled upward. "Then one day Uncle Steven took me far out on the water. So far we couldn't see the shore. It was like we had the whole lake to ourselves. He said, 'The world can't touch us out here.' He put his arm around my shoulder and held me close…then closer. Everything changed that day." Paphian drifted off. He blinked rapidly.

Edress remained steadfast. "Will you confess?"

"I'll be in jail the rest of my life."

"What do you have to live for anyway?"

Tears spilled down Paphian's cheeks.

Edress left with a surety in her heart of a positive outcome.

The next morning Edress moved back to her own

apartment and immediately started packing. David had proposed. They would marry in a month. Connie agreed to be maid of honor in a tone of mixed surprised, happiness, envy and sadness. Edress' mom couldn't wait to make the dresses, although unsure of where to purchase the fabric now.

The following afternoon David arrived at Edress' apartment looking perplexed. "Edress, sit down." They moved a box and sat close on the sofa. David took Edress' hand, "Paphian killed himself last night." He waited for a reaction.

Edress sat stunned a few seconds, then asked, "How?"

"He opened his IV and the medicine flowed freely into his veins and killed him."

"How do they know it was a suicide?"

"He left an apology letter for the molestations and a list of girls he molested. It was a long list."

"Was my name on it?"

"Yes. So was Sarah's."

PROLOGUE

A wonderful, serene year had passed since Paphian's suicide. Their first anniversary imminent, Edress and David were considering parenthood. Edress had become used to David's little quirks, like insisting the toothpaste be kept only on the second shelf of the medicine cabinet, always vacuuming before dusting, and always writing drafts before even the simplest letter to his mom.

Edress was so in love, she would sometimes just sit and watch David's movements.

This night Edress watched from their darkened foyer as David threw papers into the fireplace. The paper edges started to crinkle and burn. David looked around surreptitiously, then moved silently into the bathroom and started the shower.

Edress moved curiously to the fireplace. She knelt and snatched the paper from its fiery death. It was a letter. She unfolded the page and caught her breath sharply. Plopping back onto the rug she read,

"Dear Sarah,

You've played an important part in bringing your molester to justice. Your portrayal at Edress' home inspired her to pursue him.

I know you didn't mean to injure Edress with the car, but it worked out even better than I had planned. The hospital stay enabled us to pull off an undetectable performance. Your testimony to the police was essential. Although she never would have suspected me, Edress would have been unsure who assaulted her, and she would not have taken revenge against Paphian for this act. He could have gone unpunished.

It gives me much joy to know my little manipulations helped bring him to his knees. I could go on no longer, knowing this molester was in the community. I have heard many young girls' experiences at his hands.

Please use your payoff money wisely and do not contact me in any way. Have a good life from here forward. I wish you the best of luck in your future endeavors.

Sincerely,
David

Edress threw the letter back into the flames and sat there for what seemed an eternity.

The workings of the human heart are the profoundest mystery of the universe. One moment they make us despair of our kind, and the next we see in them the reflection of the divine image.

Charles W. Chestnut (1858-1932)
***The Marrow of Tradition* (1901)**

INSULT AND INJURY

Shuffling up to the nurses' station, I identified myself, "I'm Detective Brimley of the One-five. Where can I find Mr and Mrs Stanley Studley?" My gold shield flashed in the nurse's glasses.

"They were just brought in. You better wait 'til the doctors are through."

I peered between the ER curtains at a bloody couple in their early fifties.

The balding man lay sprawled on his side. His belly hung low over the stretcher edge. Blood spatters covered his shoulders and arms. His white (and now red) shirt lay on the floor beside him. It had been ripped open where wisps of thread replaced missing buttons. A spittle of dried blood ran from his ear onto his flushed cheek. One brown loafer was missing, revealing small lumpy toes, each trying to run from the other. The other shoe dangled perilously from his left foot.

The tiny woman's grey hair was matted to her sweaty forehead. Her shaky hand revealed blue-black facial bruises. Her other arm bent at a disturbingly weird angle ending in limp fingers with broken, unpolished nails. The pointer finger dripped blood where the nail was broken well below the skin.

The doctors flurried in, whisking each victim to an emergency station. Muffled voices ordered and responded as the two were treated with efficient emergency room urgency.

"We're putting them into Room 324, but they're asleep. Both of 'em were given pain killers." The nurse adjusted her glasses and turned back to her paperwork.

"That's alright. I'll wait around a while." I did the famous Brimley shuffle down to 324 hoping this would be a quick one. Only six months till I retired, and the boredom was killing me. You'd think all I was good for was follow up! Those young golden boys get all the juicy cases. Just because I have a little gut and grey hair is no reason to put me out to stud. And no way would I win the department's Weirdest Case Contest! This month's bet was a case of good scotch.

I eased my massive physique into the antiseptic room.

Mrs Studley's head was wrapped mummy-like with white gauze. Grey tufts stuck out the top like crabgrass. She slept soundly, exhaling little bird-like noises. Even under the sheets you could tell she weighed only about 100 pounds. Her eyes were dark and puffed closed. One casted arm hung in traction.

As Mr Studley stirred, his sheets shifted revealing a bandaged arm. His heavily casted right foot swung midair from a small trapeze. A cotton puff foamed from his left ear.

I creaked into the visitor's chair pulling a notepad from my inner trench coat pocket and made some quick notes: Mr Stanley Studley and wife, Emma. Apparent assault victims. Reason for assault: unknown. Found in hallway outside their apartment 3 p.m. by magazine solicitor. No signs of forced entry.

Mr Studley's eyes fluttered, alerting me. Slowly pushing myself up from the chair, I scuffed my way to the bed. "Mr Studley?"

Stanley gazed wide-eyed around the room, moving only his eyes. He squinched painfully as he pushed up on his elbows for a better view. "Where am I?" he whispered.

"County Memorial."

"I guess she won." Stanley said downheartedly.

"Who won what? I frowned.

"Where is she? Where's my Emma?"

"Right there." I jerked my head toward the other

bed.

"So she didn't win! Thank God. I'd never hear the end of it."

Stanley closed his eyes smiling with satisfaction.

"Wake up!" I stepped up the questioning. "Mr Studley I need to know what happened."

Dreamily Stanley murmured, "She was the sweetest thing I'd ever seen. When we met, I knew I wanted to take care of Emma the rest of her life. She felt the same about me."

"That's great Mr Studley, but what happened today?"

As if talking to himself, Stanley continued. "While hiking on our honeymoon, I cut my leg on a rock. The infection kept me in bed for weeks. Emma nursed me 24 hours a day. She enjoyed it. I did the same for her when she had walking pneumonia. We were never closer..."

"Mr Studley," I interrupted holding back a growl. "I need to get on with this investigation. Who did this to you?

"Our happiest times were when we nurtured each other through illnesses. Our marriage would have been dull without them." He winced folding his arms over his protruding belly contentedly.

"Hey Stan! Am I getting through to you? Maybe I should call a doctor."

"We went through some scary months when we thought we'd fallen out of love. We didn't need each other anymore. That's when the competition began."

I turned toward the door to find the Doc. *This guy's delirious!*

Stanley mused on. "One afternoon on the way to the store, I just pushed Emma down the stairs. It was so easy. She broke her leg. I got to take care of her for months. It was great. It renewed our love."

I froze in the doorway, reckoning I'd heard him

wrong.

"As soon as Emma recovered, she made my favorite meal, chicken and rice. On the way to the table, she tripped spilling steaming rice on my hands. I was helpless for a month. She did everything for me. It was great."

I plunked back down into the chair, ignoring the twinge in my lower back. A drip of saliva reminded me to close my mouth.

"A month later I backed the car over Emma's foot. I really didn't see her. That one was a freebie. We milked that one for a long time."

My pen and pad dropped to the floor.

"Mr Studley, if all this happened, the hospital staff would have called the police. They keep records of repeated injuries, you know."

"We already thought of that. We're old, not dumb. We made sure we were treated at a different place each time."

"But Mr Studley…"

"Please let me finish, I'm getting sleepy." His eyes were closing, but his mouth kept going. "We each wanted to care for the other. We competed to see who would get the privilege next. Emma stabbed me with a pencil, but she forgot pencils aren't made with lead anymore," he chuckled. "I didn't get infected. She was so disappointed. I dropped our penny jar on her hand. Broke three fingers with that one," he grinned wanly.

"Emma poisoned the soup one night. I was sick as a dog for a week. Maybe we got a little carried away this time. We both wanted to win so badly." Studley paused.

"Are you telling me you and your wife did this to each other!?" My mouth was gaping again.

"It's so disappointing. Now a nurse has to take care of us."

*****

Two weeks later the old One-five was buzzing along as usual, when I got the saddest call of my life. Sergeant Brandt's gruff voice boomed thought the receiver, "Just thought you'd like to know about the Studleys."

"What? Are they fighting again?"

"No. Dead"

"How?" I asked, but somehow already knew.

"They shot each other. Seemed like a mutual homicide. Why would anyone do something like that? If you hate each other that much, just get divorced."

"But what if it's love?" I told him the whole bizarre story.

The scotch was smooth.

In the part of this universe that we know there is great injustice, and often the good suffer, and often the wicked prosper, and one hardly knows which of those is the more annoying.

Bertrand Russell (1872 - 1970)

THE MINI MURDERS

He found her lying under a pile of crushed hubcaps in the filthy back corner of the Rags to Riches junkyard on Jeliff Avenue. Alerted by the incessant barking of a pack of mangy dogs, he discovered them digging into the hubcaps, like miners looking for gold. He found what appeared to be a doll. Investigating closer, he discovered the child.

Maya gasped at the morbid scene on the television, as she viewed the junk dealer standing stiffly, his torn, plaid jacket flapping in the cold wind. Behind him an EMS worker was carrying a small wrapped bundle, presumably the baby.

Why do I watch the news at breakfast? This is not the way to start the day.

Maya reluctantly watched on. Detective Morton "Pepper" Brimley was handling the case. They flashed a recent Sears Baby portrait of pretty Anne Booknight. She, indeed, looked like a doll. She couldn't have been more than a year old. Her reddish-brown ringlets framed her chubby cheeks.

Anne was found wearing a patched dress, red and white striped tights, and black Mary Janes. Her parents, who had reported her missing three days ago, did not recognize the clothes. She had been suffocated.

Two babies in one month. What's going on in Newark? Maya shook her head and switched off the television. *I just bought a hubcap from that junkyard. I wonder if the child was there then.* Maya shuddered and headed out the door.

A short two weeks ago a lady had tripped over a wet plastic bag on McWhorter Street. Cindy Rand was found in front of the Newark Gold Charm Company. She lay in the doorway in a frilly blue and white party dress. She wore clear "jelly" shoes on her tiny feet. When her body was removed by the EMTs, four dead mice were found underneath. Her stepmother was brought in for questioning.

Maya had read the story in the Newark Star Ledger. They profiled Detective "Pepper" Brimley, stating he had an emotional investment in the case. Five years ago he lost a baby in a kidnapping case. He would have been able to save the child, if he had followed up all the given clues. He ignored a few as crackpot complaints. They were the wrong few. He's never forgiven himself, though his superiors and fellow officers supported his investigation as thorough.

Brimley's picture accompanied the article. He was a round, rumpled man with a medium complexion, thick furry mustache and balding head. He looked like he should be running a newsstand, not an investigation.

Maya Willis shuffled carefully through the snow from the very last spot in the parking lot behind her job. Even with her head down against the icy wind, the snow blasted her cheeks. *Why am I always the last one to get to work in bad weather? I don't live that far away. Thank goodness it's Friday.* She pulled her woolen scarf over her mouth and nose, and squinted her eyes against the cold. As she rounded the side of the dingy red brick building and cut across the whitened lawn to save time. Maya tripped and fell headlong into the high drifts sloped against the walls. "What the hell?" She knelt, and then rose unsteadily, leaning against the snowy wall. *What's this?* Annoyed, Maya kicked the small hill of packed snow at her feet. It slid a couple of inches on the ice. Maya bent to look closer. She halted inches away.

A half hour later Detective Brimley entered the White Ruby Company to see a shaken Maya Willis cowering in the lunchroom corner. A uniformed female officer was by her side. Lumbering across the room, Brimley carefully settled his bulk into one of plastic chairs next to Maya. "Miss Willis, I need you to tell me what happened."

Maya relayed the morning's events to Brimley. He listened, sometimes intently, sometimes gazing upward, seemingly lost in personal thought. He wrapped up the interview, snapped his pad shut and waddled out the door. Maya went home to recuperate.

Saturday morning Maya felt better. She hurried down Broad Street toward The Fairy's Closet, a popular children's clothing store. She had begged for the honor of buying her nephew's party outfit. It was Petey's first birthday. Although Maya never wanted babies of her own, she was thrilled with the births of her sister, Gwen's, children. Maya had an eight-by-ten picture in her living room of Petey when he was brought home from the hospital wearing a green Jets cap Russell had bought him. She enjoyed reading to four-year-old Sherri, who had already developed an affinity for books. Every time she visited, Sherri would pull out her favorite fairy tale book and beg Maya to read a story. Maya took great pleasure in the fact Sherri loved that book over the dozens of others in her growing library, because it was the one she bought her.

Maya walked into the brightly lit cheeriness of the Fairy's Closet. The walls were covered with a mural of fairy tale characters, hand-painted by Luella herself. The register had helium balloons floating above it. There were two shelves of children's books behind the counter. The linoleum floor sported a bright pink, blue and yellow daisy pattern. Maya loved this store. She'd been buying children's clothes here since her niece was born. The owner, Luella, lived in the apartment above the store. The first few customers were mulling about, picking colorful clothes off the racks. Maya strode to the register, "Hi Luella."

Luella pushed her reading glasses down her round nose and peered over them at Maya. She laid down her shiny letter opener and broke out in a big smile, "Hi Maya. How ya been?" Her Texas twang always cracked Maya up.

Luella was a skinny chocolate brown woman with short cropped, curly, dark brown hair. Although only in her early thirties, her big, sad eyes portrayed an age beyond her years.

Maya had given Luella the extra sharp letter opener as a token Christmas gift last year. She had merely recycled an unwanted birthday gift, but Luella gushed excitedly when she received it.

Ya lookin' for somethin' special today?" Luella leaned over the counter and gave Maya a big kiss on her cheek, leaving a greasy, red smudge. Maya wore the same shade, but it didn't look as brassy as it did on Luella.

"Yeah. My nephew will be one year old soon. I'm buying him an outfit for his first birthday party."

"Really? That's great. When's the party?"

"In two weeks, on Saturday."

Luella scrawled the date on her personalized Fairy's Closet memo pad. The tag line read "For the little joys in your life".

"Where are the best party clothes?"

Luella pointed to the left corner of the room and went back to opening her mail.

A half hour later Maya bounced out of the store with a matching Cross Colours pullover shirt and denim pants.

Maya was just sitting down to dinner when the doorbell rang. Detective Brimley lumbered in and stood awkwardly in the foyer. He held a large manila envelope under his arm. "Miss Willis, I'm sorry to intrude on your evening, but I have a few more questions."

Maya led him into the living room. Brimley settled into her plump, taupe lounge chair. Between Brimley's bulk and his rumpled trench coat, one couldn't tell where the chair ended and Brimley began. Maya sat stiffly on the edge of her white jacquard sofa opposite him. He laid the envelope on the oak coffee table between them.

"Now Miss Willis, these are photos of the baby you found," he cautioned. "I want you to take a close look and tell me if you recognize this child."

"Do I have to look?" Maya put her hand on her throat and turned away.

"Please. I know it's not a pleasant task, but it may help the investigation."

Time expanded while Maya lifted the envelope by one corner with two fingers. Hands shaking, she bent the flap back and pulled out the photos. There in the snow lay a frozen child. Her skin was porcelain white. Her ebony curls were framed by a bright red headband, topped with a tiny bow. The puff sleeves of her fancy blue and yellow dress were stiffened with frost and smeared with a greasy red substance. Her tiny mouth was smudged cartoon-like with bright red lipstick.

Maya dropped the photos, ran to the bathroom and vomited.

Sunday morning Maya drove to church, for the first time in months. She needed to be around people and God. Driving down South Orange Avenue, she seemed to see babies everywhere, mothers with strollers, fathers carrying snowsuited babies, grandmothers lifting young ones out of rear car seats. She was grateful to pull onto Springfield Avenue and reach the Miracle Baptist church.

After an uplifting service, Maya walked to the parking lot along with the throngs of worshippers. Some people gathered in gossipy little cliques. Others strolled to their cars. The afternoon sun was melting the snow. Serenity surrounded Maya for the first time since Friday's shock.

Maya drove toward Gwen and Russell's house in Vailsburg to invite herself to Sunday dinner. They never minded when she did this, and it was a good thing too, for she did it often.

Turning onto Richelieu Terrace, Maya remembered how Gwen and Russell tried desperately for five years before Gwen became pregnant with Sherri. Then it took another four years before Petey came along. Gwen was unable to conceive more children which made the two they had the most precious gifts on earth.

Gwen opened the front door of their large old Tudor home. "Hey, Sis!" She swept Maya up in her arms for a warm sisterly hug. "I guess you just dropped by in time for dinner?" Gwen tilted her head and raised one eyebrow comically. They both laughed and meandered into the living room.

Maya plopped down on the worn couch, barely missing a Barney toy. She kicked aside some building blocks and stretched out her legs. "Mmmm, something smells good. What are we having?"

"Fried chicken, black eyed peas and rice. You didn't happen to bring dessert, did you?"

"Oops, next time sis." Maya rolled her eyes upward and grinned sheepishly. "I know that's our deal, dinner for dessert. Sue me, if you can find an honest lawyer."

When the laughter settled, Maya sighed, "I've really had a rough week."

"What happened?"

Maya chronicled Friday's episode.

After dinner, Maya read a story out of the Famous Fairy Tales book to Sherri. Petey sat on her lap trying to turn pages with sticky fingers. Sherri sat on the floor, coughing every few minutes.

Gwen entered the room, "Sherri, put on your slippers and sit on the couch." She put her hand on Sherri's forehead with a concerned look.

"Does she have a cold?" Maya asked frowning.

"Didn't you hear her coughing all through dinner? It's a good thing you don't have kids."

"Does she have a virus or something?" Maya asked a little ashamed for not noticing.

"The doctor said she should be alright. She's taking antibiotics and staying warm," her voice rose, "and not sitting on the floor." Turning back to Sherri, "What did I just tell you?"

Sherri jumped up and ran to get her slippers.

Maya returned to church for evening service. As she parked her car, Maya noticed a large crowd gathering in the empty lot behind the Wonderland Bakery across the street from the church. Police car lights sparked red and blue in the night.

As if drawn by an invisible thread, Maya crossed the street and wandered into the crowd. A man was kneeling in the melting snow. A small blue and white fabric pile lay at his feet. Moving closer Maya could see a baby in a blue dress with a little white-bibbed apron. A blue ribbon was tied around her head through her little blonde curls. Brightly painted red lips stood stark against pale skin. Her white tights were covered in crumbs. The man slowly turned his head and looked Maya in the eyes. He stood. Red, blue, red, blue. The lights flashed on Detective Brimley's stern face.

Maya's blood iced. Everything faded except Brimley's eyes.

That night Maya awaited the doorbell jangle. Brimley accommodated her. She opened the door to see Brimley waiting on the porch minus his previous awkwardness.

"Miss Willis, I'd like you to come downtown with me. We'd like to ask you a few questions."

Maya glanced over his shoulder to see a uniformed officer waiting in a police car at the curb. "Why do I have to go downtown? Can't we talk here?"

"We just need your help, Ma'am. Will you come down voluntarily?" Brimley stated more like an order than a request.

The precinct, though modern, was still creepy. Maya glanced around warily half afraid, half ashamed to be there. She sat alone in a small room with only a table and a few hard wooden chairs. Past the closed door a cacophony of scary, unfamiliar noises reduced Maya to childlike fright, reminiscent of nights spent fearing the boogeyman in the closet. Brimley walked in and hovered over her. He had removed the now-familiar rumpled trench coat to reveal a round belly sagging over wrinkled corduroy pants. A silent minute felt like an hour of anxiety.

"Now Miss Willis, you have been at the location of other murders. Why is that?"

"What do you mean 'other murders'? I just happen to go to the Miracle Church. Lots of people go to that church."

"What I don't understand is why you would allow yourself to be seen. Do you think you're that clever?"

"W-w-what? You can't think I did this. I love children."

"Really? How many children do you have?"

"None. I'm not married."

"That doesn't stop women nowadays."

"Well, it stops me." Maya would have been indignant if she weren't so frightened.

Brimley paced around the pitted table, then leaned on it directly opposite Maya. His coal-black eyes looked directly into Maya's wide brown ones. "Miss Willis, a woman of your description has also been seen at the scene of another murder."

"W-w-what?" Maya paused to compose herself. "What do you mean a woman of my description? Where?"

"Do you deny visiting the Newark Gold Charm Company?"

Maya tried unsuccessfully to calm herself. *How could I have forgotten?* Maya had purchased a charm bracelet for Sherri as a get well gift. The charms represented healing flowers such as chamomile, alfalfa, and red clover. Maya wished she had some chamomile right now.

"Don't bother thinking up an excuse. We already know you were there," Brimley growled. He continued to circle Maya, spiraling closer as he stepped.

"Miss Willis, I caution you to tell the truth now. If you lie, things will become rough for you."

"I've been telling the truth." Maya rose slightly from her chair.

"Sit down!" Brimley barked.

Maya fell back on the hard wood seat. She blinked back fearful tears.

"Have you ever been to the Rags to Riches Junkyard?"

The world stopped. Maya's eyes darted back and forth like a trapped animal. If allowed, she would have paced in her cage. In a tiny, child-like voice Maya said, "Yes."

The journey into Hell began.

After three hours of repeated questioning, Brimley released Maya with the promise of future interviews. A uniformed officer dropped Maya at her front door. Tired and shaken Maya sat heavily on her sofa and stared into space with red-rimmed eyes. The evening had a supernatural feel to it. Maya's mind raced. *I can't believe they think I could kill a baby. Should I get a lawyer? I don't have any money. Who can I talk to? Maybe they'll find the real killer. Thousands of innocent people are sent to jail.* Maya's thoughts followed her into sleep.

Before fully awakening, Maya had an ominous feeling about the day. After a quick shower, she sat at her kitchen table and sipped a hot cup of coffee. *I may need an attorney, but that takes cash, and I sure don't have any.* Her eyes rolled about as her mind reviewed her measly bank accounts and her possessions. With a sudden surge of energy, Maya ran into her living room and began rummaging in her coat closet.

A half hour later Maya arrived at the Forest Fur Company. A half bald, half gray white man approached the door as she entered. He swept his deeply veined hand toward a tall clothing rack. Maya hung her full-length fox coat on it. A few moments later she left, check in hand.

The telephone jangled urgently. "What time is it?" Maya fumbled for the alarm clock on her nightstand and rubbed her eyes to clear the sleep. Three a.m. She grabbed the phone, almost knocking over the lamp. "Hello?"

"Maya, it's me, Gwen. Sherri's really sick. We're at University Hospital. We think she has pneumonia." Gwen sniffed, "Please come down to the hospital."

Fifteen minutes later Maya raced into the emergency room. She located Gwen and Russell standing stiffly outside a curtained-off room. Russell held Gwen closely as she wept quietly. Maya slowed her pace and breathing.

"Gwen, what's going on?"

"The doctor said it's more than pneumonia. She got sick so fast."

Gwen seemed to shrink as the doctor pulled back the curtain and approached them. He spoke without looking them in the eye.

"Mr. and Mrs. Wilkes, I'm sorry. Your daughter had a fatal form of meningitis. She succumbed more quickly than expected. We were unable to help her."

Gwen swooned into Russell's chest. Three adults cried like children.

It was the saddest funeral of all. A grief-stricken Gwen almost missed the services. The church was packed with solemn faces. Shaking heads bemoaned disbelief at the death of one so young.

Maya sat silently next to her sister and brother-in-law in the front pew. She was torn between supporting Gwen and drowning in grief. Maya passed the morning in a dreamlike haze barely noticing Pepper Brimley's silent vigil from the last pew.

Later at home Maya sat at her kitchen table disoriented and emotionally drained since returning from the funeral. Out of habit, she flipped on the television. The six o'clock news was just coming on. *Some chamomile tea might knock me out for a while.* She rose and filled her teapot with spring water.

The newscasters buzzed on in the background of her thoughts until she heard the words "Forest Fur Company".

"After a two day search, Eleven month old Sashi Sanjay was found behind the Forest Fur Company on Market Street in Newark," the newscaster droned. "This is the fifth baby connected to what has now been dubbed as the 'Mini Murders'. Sashi wore a fringed, tan dress. Her ebony hair was frozen in the snow. Her bronze skin was bruised about the cheeks..."

Maya's teapot crashed to the linoleum. Water

splayed out over her stocking feet. As the panic rose in her chest, she knew one thing. She would have to prove her innocence.

Ignoring the mess on the floor, Maya ran upstairs to her bedroom and packed hurriedly. She grabbed her stash of cash, (a whole $100), her credit cards and cell phone.

After a quick stop at the automatic teller, Maya raced to the Best Western Hotel near the Newark Airport. She checked in, paying cash. As soon as she locked her door, she collapsed in exhaustion on the bed.

Nine hours later, Maya awakened and lay a moment taking in her surroundings. She pushed herself up from the bed and started toward the bathroom. Passing the dresser mirror, she noted her lipstick was smeared onto her cheek. Maya froze at the sight.

Maya stared into the mirror horror-struck. The one thing the murdered babies had in common was red lipstick! At least the two babies she had seen. But there was something else familiar; the way an old odor sticks to your memory. She could almost touch the thought… almost.

After refreshing her makeup and quickly changing her clothes, Maya drove two miles, arriving at a beat up phone booth in a liquor store parking lot on the highway. She dropped a quarter into the slot and after three rings, Gwen answered her cell phone.

"Where are you?" Gwen whispered. "That fat detective was looking for you."

"What did he say?" Maya echoed Gwen's whisper.

"He says you're a suspect in those baby murders, and you have to turn yourself in. They got a search warrant and searched your house. They took your computer, some papers and something strange."

"What?"

"They were looking for your makeup."

"I think I know why. Gwen, you know I couldn't possibly hurt a child. Please keep your faith in me."

"Always."

Maya returned to her hotel room to ponder the situation. *Hopefully some ginseng tea will help the process. There's something about these babies that's familiar.*

Maya sat at the desk and drew the complimentary writing pad and pen toward her. Drawing a grid, she charted the known facts about each murder. Names, locations, clothing, anything she could think of. *I have to find a pattern.* She then placed the little victims in order of the murders. *Mini Murders*, she thought. Fleeting glimpses of something familiar darted through her brain, then suddenly, a flash of clear cognizance.

"Fairy tales!" Maya shouted. Startled by her own voice, she almost knocked over her ginseng.

Back at the phone booth, Maya spoke excitedly to Gwen. "Don't you see? The babies are dressed in fairytale costumes. The girl found in the junk yard was Raggedy Anne. The one found on McWhorter Street was Cinderella."

Gwen hesitated, "Well, I don't know."

"It's got to be. I discovered Snow White near my job. I saw Alice in Wonderland across from my church," Maya's voice escalated. "The baby found at Forest Fur was Pocahontas!"

Caught up in the excitement Gwen practically yelled, "Just like in Sherri's book!"

Both ends of the phone line silenced. Gwen began to weep silently. Maya stood stunned.

After thirty seconds of dead air, Maya said, "Get the book." After a short conversation, Maya hung up and clinked another quarter into the slot.

"Brimley here," he said abruptly.

Maya quickly explained her theory.

Brimley paused, then said, "Turn yourself in Ms Willis. If you make us hunt you down, we'll be much harder on you."

"But aren't you listening? There's a serial killer out there living out fairy tales!"

"Now you listen! We already figured that out. We're way ahead of you. The fact that you know the pattern makes you even more of a suspect. Tell me where you are and ..."

Maya banged the phone into its hook and ran to her car. Chances were she was being traced. She had to move.

Maya rapidly repacked her bag, checked out of the fabulous Best Western, hopped into her well-worn Toyota, and drove to Satellite Motors on McCarter Highway. After some fast talking, she drove out with a used pale yellow Volkswagen.

Maya parked in one of the many huge Newark Airport parking lots. She walked into the Jersey Diner located in terminal C and took a seat near the back. She ordered a cup of chamomile tea and some blueberry pie. Then pulled out the rumpled murder chart and studied it again. *Gwen was right. The fairy tales match the book. The murders even happened in the same order as the stories in the book. But the last story was missing. Peter Pan. That means another murder will take place!*

Calling Brimley was out of the question. If Maya predicted another murder, he'd put out an all points bulletin for her. "Famous Fairy Tales" was the key.

The next two nights Maya slept in her car, starting at every passing pedestrian or vehicle.

Monday morning Maya called Gwen at work from an airport phone booth. "Don't say my name."

"Believe me I won't. Detective Brimley has men watching both our houses. I think my home phone is tapped. He said he knows you're the murderer because he matched your lipstick to lipstick found on all the babies."

"But lots of women wear that color."

"You're the only one linked to the murders."

"I can name several women I know who wear that lipstick. Even…"

"Maya?"

"I've got to go!" Maya hung up abruptly. *I know what I have to do.*

Maya entered the enormous entryway of the Newark Public Library. She went to the second floor archive room and began poring over old newspaper articles of kidnapped and murdered children. After two and a half hours she struck gold.

A special article had been written on kidnapped and murdered children of Newark which listed names and dates. Using this information Maya began tediously finding and printing accounts of the murders. She was printing the twelfth article when she heard a familiar grumble.

"Where is she?"

A mousy voice stage whispered, "She's by the printer. She's been there for hours. I thought it seemed strange and with the recent murders, I thought I should alert the police…"

Snatching her jacket from the chair, Maya ran behind the stacks and down the back stairs clutching her precious printouts. She ran to her car and sped away.

Maya's funds were getting low, but she managed to find a cheap, clean motel on route 9 and settled in. Spreading the printouts over the worn bedcover she perused them intently. The details were sketchy, but the similarities were startling.

At least three articles noted red lipstick on a baby's face. Four revealed the costumes worn. Although names were not specified, by description Maya knew they were

Alice in Wonderland, Cinderella, Pocahontas and Raggedy Anne. The murders had been going on for years… and none were solved.

The twelfth article was very old. It was about a young girl named Luella who was kidnapped from her birth mother at the age of ten. Her "new mother" held her in a tenement with no heat or hot water. Luella was forced to do all the housework and cooking.

Men frequented the household and when they wanted to stay, little Luella's mother would lock her away "for her own safety" in a filthy room for days at a time with no food or water. The only refuge Luella had from the grunts heard through her thin bedroom walls was her fairy tale book. She would sit on her twin bed, cover her ears and read the book over and over.

One of the men actually had a conscience and alerted the police to the situation. There was a picture of police escorting a small, unkempt girl away from a rotting slum. Held tight in her arms was a large book.

Maya sat in stunned silence. She almost felt sorry for her…almost.

Maya lay low for the evening. She left the room once to grab some fast food, ate hurriedly and fell into a fitful sleep. The next morning she called Gwen's cell phone.

A frightened voice answered the phone, "Yes?"

"What's wrong?" Maya's sister-sense alerted her to the distress.

"P-P-Petey's gone."

"What do you mean 'gone'?" Maya held her breath.

"He was taken while I was in the grocery store. I turned my back for a few seconds. When I turned around he was…gone." Gwen's voice hitched.

Maya's blood iced. Her lungs froze.

"You know, after Sherri's funeral I could barely

get out of bed for weeks."

Maya nodded unseen. She knew Gwen had only been able to face the world in tiny phases. Then she began to mend her broken heart by pouring love over little Petey. Nothing was too good for him.

"Russell and I had decided to go ahead with Petey's belated birthday party. We thought maybe what's left of our family, could begin to heal."

Maya felt sick. Her stomach churned crazily.

"Maya, there's more."

"What?"

"Brimley was here. He thinks you're involved." There was a brief silence on Gwen's end of the phone as if she were considering the possibility.

"Are you waiting for me to respond to that?" Maya was amazed.

"Please, Maya, if you know anything, you've got to help us."

"Just hold on Sis. I'll take care of this," Maya slammed down the receiver.

That night Maya drove downtown and parked on Branford Place near the abandoned Branford Theater. The stores were closed. Only the local taverns and restaurants were still open. Maya pulled on a black skullcap and swept up the hood of her black microfiber sweatshirt. The wind whipped about her. With head down she traversed the back alley past disgusting dumpsters leading to the Fairy's Closet. Maya shivered at the thought her nephew could have been taken into this filthy darkness.

She approached the back door of the store and peered side to side. Nothing moved except wind blown papers and a few passing cars. Maya pulled an old, but reliable Coleman flashlight from her sweatshirt pocket. She looked around once more to ensure there would be no interference. She shined the light on the building. A rusty wire gate with a heavy padlock covered the back door.

Both windows were blocked by steel rods like an old western jailhouse. Maya tested the padlock just for her peace of mind. Of course, it was locked. She waved the light beam over the second story. There were two small windows about a foot over a small ledge. *I guess this is as good as it gets,* Maya thought.

Maya shivered as she crept over to the wheeled dumpster behind the Fairy's Closet. Using all of her strength, she pushed it against the wall under the two windows. The squealing wheels made Maya shiver more than the dumpster's cold steel. She shoved the flashlight into her pocket and climbed onto the dumpster guided by moonlight. Sticking her toes into the first floor window grates, she hoisted herself up and grabbed a rusty drainpipe for balance. Maya inched up the grates until she was able to reach up and touch the ledge above. With all her strength she held on and swung one leg up onto the ledge. It took two full minutes for her to pull her entire body onto the ledge.

Maya rested for a moment, listening for any movement. Sweat stung her eyes despite the cold. In the silence she pulled the flashlight out of her pocket and beamed it into a small six-paned window.

The room was empty, the door closed. Replacing the flashlight into her pocket, Maya pushed upward against the window with the heels of her hands. No movement. Maya took a deep breath and pushed with all of her one hundred twenty pounds. The window opened with a crackle of breaking ice. Maya practically fell into the room.

She stood cautiously, again listening for signs of life. Nothing. She relit the Coleman and swept the room with light.

The room was pale yellow with a slanted ceiling. There was a mural on the walls depicting fairy tale characters. Maya's mouth dropped open as she surveyed the walls. *Just like in the store. Raggedy Ann, Cinderella, Snow White, Alice in Wonderland, Pocahontas, Peter Pan.*

A twin sized bed with a thin, ruffled coverlet filled one corner. Otherwise the room seemed barren. Maya slowly covered the room with the dim flashlight beam. Peeping out from underneath the ruffled bedspread was a box. *No, it's a book.*

Maya bent and pulled it out. Turning the flashlight to the cover, she stopped breathing. It was a well worn copy of Famous Fairy Tales. Plopping down on the bed, Maya laid the book on her lap and opened the cover. Slowly, she turned the familiar pages.

At the beginning of the first story, Raggedy Ann, were scrawled notes. At first Maya couldn't make them out. Then she realized it was a list of names. Maya tried to wet her forefinger, but had no spit. She began flipping the pages faster. Cinderella, Snow White, Alice in Wonderland, Pocahontas, Peter Pan. Each had a list of names on the first story page. The last story, Peter Pan, had a list of four names. Maya's eyes widened. She gasped at the name…Peter Wilkes.

Maya jumped to her feet, banging the book to the floor. Again she froze listening for sounds. With her toe, she carefully pushed the book back under the bed. Then…a muffled moan. She tilted her head. Again, a moan, this time accompanied with soft thumps.

Quietly, Maya advanced to the door and cracked it open. The sounds became louder. They emanated from the lower floor. She crept down the hall to the stairwell. Reaching the first floor, Maya stopped again. The sounds continued, much louder. The latch snapped open easily, and much too loudly for Maya's taste. She entered the store level from the rear.

Lit by the streetlights the fairy tale characters on the walls looked eerie at night. Their eyes followed her everywhere. The thumping had stopped. Maya couldn't risk using, her faithful Coleman near the huge display windows of the Fairy's Closet. So she stuck it in the front pocket of her sweatshirt.

Maya hunched low and tiptoed around the room, ducking behind racks as she traveled. There was no place to hide in the open space. Then by the streetlights glow she spotted two doors in the right rear corner. One, she knew, led to the dressing room. The other she supposed was storage.

Maya entered the storage closet and closed the door behind her. She felt the wall near the door until she found the light switch. Maya squinted as the overhead light flashed on. It illuminated the small, cluttered room fully. Racks of plastic covered clothing lined three walls. Miscellaneous supply boxes were stacked on shelves at the far end of the room. There on the floor was a burlap duffle bag. It moved…and moaned.

Quickly Maya knelt down and untied the tightly knotted cord to reveal a half-conscious Petey. His tiny face was slightly bruised and he breathed in little hitches.

Tears rolled down Maya's face as she pulled Petey from the rough sack and gathered him into her arms. As she wiped the tears from her eyes, she first noticed the strange pajamas he wore; brown stretch pants, a green pajama shirt and tan booties. *What the…?*

On instinct Maya reached into the duffle bag and felt around. At the bottom of the bag was piece de resistance. She pulled out a green felt cap which sported a red feather on one side. It was the final piece to a Peter Pan costume!

Terror reemerged from Maya's heart. Standing unsteadily, she lifted Petey over her shoulder and turned to leave the room. As Maya flicked off the light, a bright glare shone from underneath the door. Footsteps. Paper shuffling.

Maya held her breath. Petey coughed. The shuffling stopped. Maya's tightened stomach muscles made her ribs ache. The light went out. Then, a door slam. Maya released a swooshing breath. She cautiously opened the door and stepped into the store.

Maya tiptoed unsteadily, balancing Petey's weight on one shoulder. As she reached the middle of the room, the lights flashed on. Maya almost dropped Petey as she swerved around to see Luella standing near the door to her residence, arms crossed.

Luella moved swiftly to Maya. She uncrossed her arms to reveal the long, slender letter opener. It glinted in the fluorescents as she twisted it back and forth in the air.

"I see you've found my little dreamboat," Luella smiled.

"Stay away from us, Luella," Maya whispered. "I'm on to you and so are the police."

"The police think you're the killer. I made sure of that," Luella grinned even wider.

Maya's eyes widened. She almost forgot her precious cargo. "What do you mean?"

"You were the perfect target. You're a loner with no children. I easily planted Snow White at your job."

"How did you know someone else wouldn't find her?"

"I waited until I saw you pull into the parking lot. You're always late on snowy days. You told me yourself. You see, that's what made you an easy target. You'd come in every few months to buy something for your little darlings. You'd tell me you were going to the junkyard to replace your lost hubcap. Or you'd mention some church function."

"I hadn't been to church in months," Maya answered with a mix of anger and shame.

"Yeah, I took a chance on that one. I figured finding Snow White at your job might drive you to service. I watched your house that Sunday and followed you to church."

"How do you know where I live?" Maya responded horrified.

"See, that's what I mean about you. You have been on my mailing list for four years." Luella inched closer. "Most of the women who shop here just buy clothes and leave. You took the time to chat and treat me like a real person, not just a store clerk. You even gave me this letter opener for Christmas."

Maya backed toward the front door. "OK, I understand why you picked me, but why do you kill babies?" The phrase "kill babies" stuck in her throat.

Luella stopped moving. A painful look covered her face. "I don't kill. You can't kill fairy tales. They're not real."

Maya's mouth dropped open. "W-w-what?"

"I live for my stories. They're the only thing that keeps me going. I wait until I see my favorite fairy tale character. Then I bring them home and read them their story. When the story's done, I close the book on them.

"It's the only comfort I get in life. It's the reason I opened this shop. Women bring children here all the time. I always know when I see my fairy tale child. Raggedy Anne had red curls and a button nose. Cinderella's mom called her Cindy. Cindy lost a shoe here one day. It was a clear sign. They all give signs."

"But why Petey? You never even met him."

"He gave the strongest signals of all. You loved him so much. It was always Petey this and Petey that. You showed me the picture postcard his parents had made. It read, "Peter Wilkes born to Russell and Gwen Wilkes, yadda, yadda, yadda. Their address was on the card, too."

"But why pick him? You must have seen hundreds of baby pictures." Maya backed closer to the front door.

"It was his cap."

"His cap?"

"He was wearing a green cap. Not blue or pink as usual."

"So what?" Maya glanced back disheartened at the numerous locks on the front door.

"His name was Peter *and* he wore a green cap. The fact that you were his aunt was just gravy. It's fate for him to be Peter Pan." Luella closed in, raising the letter opener high.

Maya turned and dropped Petey by the door. The opener plunged into the back of her upper arm. Blood spread slowly into her sweatshirt. Maya screamed and fell against the glass door. Luella raised the opener again and aimed for Maya's neck.

Suddenly Luella arched her back. Her mouth hung open like a stroke victim's. Her eyes rolled back. Luella spiraled toward the back of the room and fell at Maya's feet.

Maya looked up dazed and amazed as Brimley, gun raised, entered the room from the back door. He slowly approached Luella's twisted body and kicked the bloody letter opener away. Her eyes were still open with a surprised expression.

Brimley helped Maya to her feet. Then lifted a dazed, but awakening, Petey into his arms.

"What are you doing here?" Maya asked confused, but relieved.

"I'm not as stupid as you think. I found another link to the murders... The Fairy's Closet. The babies all had links to this place. When I drove by tonight, I saw lights going on and off. I came through the back and the rest you know."

Maya said words she never imagined saying, "Thank you Detective Brimley".

"Call me Pepper," he smiled.

The morning news anchor said, "Detective Morton Brimley is declared a hero for solving the horrific Mini Murders. The Mayor's office will be honoring him with a banquet and plaque."

They showed a clip of the Mayor shaking hands with Brimley on the City Hall steps. Brimley stood stiffly in a brand new suit and tie.

Maya sat with Gwen and Russell in their living room watching the broadcast. Petey slept wedged between them on the couch. It was a good day.

Nobody is stronger...than someone who came back. There is nothing you can do to such a person because whatever you could do is less than what has already been done to him.

**Elie Wiesel
Writer .**

***

Sticks in a bundle are unbreakable.

African proverb

THE FLATTENERS

It's been centuries since we were forced underground. It's been so long that as the new generations were birthed, we developed a sonar sight which is now used more than our regular vision. We used to live in the sun and fresh air and enjoy cool raindrops on our backs and warm breezes wafting over our dark bodies.

Then one day we felt the ground rumble. We thought it was an earthquake until we spied the huge steel machines. They plowed into the earth and re-leveled it disrupting our daily routines of harvesting food and building housing for our growing population.

After years of war, we had learned to live in peace. Our armies were there only to protect us from outsiders, no longer to control or terrorize us. We ran food cooperatives to sustain our population. We built each others homes. Everyone worked, and everyone was cared for.

Our society was such that we had no survival fears. Everyone grew up knowing they would have shelter and food, you know, the basics. Some of the younger generations were beginning to take our easy existence for granted, when the machines came.

Much of our population was lost, ground mercilessly into the rich earth from which our sustenance had grown. Those who survived learned to live without the beautiful sunlight and freedom we had grown used to. Thanks to our resourceful stockpiling of food, we were able to survive underground for years.

After what seemed like an interminable cacophony of metal scraping, trees falling, rocks crunching, there came temporary peace. The machines fell silent and retreated. We peeked out of our caves and thought we were finally safe. Many of our secret doorways were blocked. As fast as we built them, our new enemies had covered them with impervious materials. We scrambled out of our hiding places into the blinding sun. Our world had changed dramatically.

Much of the soft greenery was now black or white, and hard. The structures left behind were so tall they appeared to reach into the sky. Most of our food sources were gone. The eerie silence was compounded by wind whistling between the imposing formations.

We gathered what we could and brought it into our dark warehouses, scurrying under the threat of the machines' return. We had no way to know an even worse future awaited us.

A few suns after our fleeting freedom, we poked our heads into a rainy daylight. We were searching for anything we could carry back to our silos, any greenery to keep us alive. We made the mistake of traveling far from our entryway.

As we carried the measly few greens we could find back to our pitiful abode, we heard a new, terrifying noise. The horrifying scraping sound closed in quickly. We ran as fast as possible without losing our loads. I turned just in time to see a large flat, oblong object flatten the last of us. My comrade had fallen behind. Now he lay bloodied and lifeless.

The war began. We had to survive. Even though it seemed safer to go out in the night, we older, more experienced workers could see better by day. Only our young interns could see well at night, and they didn't have our skills. We worked out schedules to ensure our safety, pairing the old and young.

Whether we went out by day or night, *the Flatteners*, as we now call them, would wipe out some of our crew. The older of our members were, of course, slower then the young ones. So they were the primary lives lost. A few young ones died. Being inexperienced in following our trails, they would get lost and wander across the stone fields often running right into *the Flatteners*.

Although our population had boomed while in hiding (After all what else is there to do in the dark?), we could not afford to lose any skilled workers. Our aboveground time was limited so as to provide only sparse times for harvest training. Many of our race were inexperienced in any useful trade.

But now we are running out of food. We are running out of patience. We have no choice but to fight back.

Night is our best time now. The younger ones use mostly sonar as they've rarely been above ground. The elders are becoming increasingly fearful of leaving the caves. Although becoming long of tooth myself, I can not stand by and see our race wiped out. My life means little if I must live in fear and watch my people choose to die by either starvation or slaughter.

That's why tonight we will attack. Our enemies are huge and powerful, but we will die if we don't fight back.

We leave our secret exits by cold moonlight. We march by the thousands, keeping close ranks so as not to lose anyone. We older ones are flanked either side by the youngsters as they have the strongest sonar. All but the babies and a few elderly are with us tonight.

Across the stone horizon we march to the front of the structure. Many of the younger ones are awed by its size and seeming dominance. Some of the youngest cry in fear.

We climb tediously up a high ledge and onto a plateau. Hundreds fit tightly here, shoulder to shoulder, in silence awaiting my signal. At the end of this level, we can see a miniscule opening. Our enemies have made a mistake.

I give the wave.

Stealthily we each bend low and squeeze into the opening. We assemble in the largest cave we have ever seen, until each and every one of us has entered.

Thousands of us, the strongest army possible, are ready to strike.

There are smaller formations inside the cave of various colors and textures. We had never seen the like. We edge further into the cave onto a fuzzy soft surface. Each step takes us further into a colorful jungle of inedible, pliable spikes. We stay close so as not to lose each other in the density of the terrain.

Some of the younger ones immediately sense food in the area. We desperately need all the food we can find, so I dispatch a battalion of one hundred to gather food and carry it back to our storage areas. Eagerly they run to the east like a black blanket of hope, wanting to be our saviors.

Our plan is to destroy the Flatteners or at the very least run them off. We stand silently listening for movement. Turning west we pick up sounds of moaning. Low, agonizing groans accompanied by high squeaking sounds and slight vibrations.

We move as one toward the sounds. As we get closer the vibrations shake our legs beneath us, but we must stay our course. I signal our army to precede our civilians into the predicted battle. They can weaken the enemy; then we can finish them off.

Yes, I know this is a very loose plan, almost no plan at all, but we have no formal knowledge of our enemy's strength or resources. This is the best we can do...and it has to work.

As we move westward, we clear the fuzzy terrain and trod onto a flat hard surface. We struggle to remain quiet, though our adversaries shouldn't hear us above their own noise. There are little patches of light peeking into the cave through openings in the cavern walls. We run through the light into the shadows where our black bodies blend with the night.

Suddenly the squeaking stops, and the groans

subside to whimpers. Our enemies reside just above us. We have reached a soft, wavering wall. Our army buzzes with excitement while our civilians shiver with a mix of anticipation and trepidation.

We are ready to meet our enemy.

The wall has little substance, but is easily scaled by the first wave of our army. How can such a soft mountain hold such powerful rivals? The first battalion has reached the top and is followed by the second and third. We, civilians, await our enemies' flight from their perch to launch an attack here below.

We hold our breath.

Suddenly we are shocked by the most horrible shrieking we have ever heard. The mountain jerks and rumbles violently. A few soldiers fall from unseen heights into our crowd, but they are strong and unhurt.

Just in time, I order our group to fall back so as not to be crushed by the Flatteners when they fall. Two Flatteners hit the ground, crushing ten of our crew. Another twenty of us jumped on top of each enemy. The Flatteners shake violently. Their shrieks grow louder. We hang on with all our strength as they swing us up into the air and violently hit the ground trying to shake us.

The Flattener's surface is softer and more vulnerable then when they attack us on our turf. It appears we have succeeded in catching them off guard, without their armor.

Suddenly we are hit with a shock of brilliant light. Colors come into focus, and we see the actual size of the devils who torture us. Even without their armor they are twenty times our length and wide enough to smash thirty of us at once. In front they have extensions of various sizes which wriggle individually. These monsters are even uglier than imaginable without their armor.

From around the other side of the mountain appears another ogre duo. They are also shaking sporadically, trying to dislodge our army fighters to no avail. Now they are the bloodied ones. As the Flatteners round the mountain, our forces split up and surround them. The four Flatteners cannot escape us now.

You see, there's a difference in physical power and power of the spirit. We will prevail because we have nothing to lose. We are fighting for our lives and the continuation our race…not to control others. The power of control is an illusion and a temporary one at that. Even if we lose this battle, we will return to win the war because we must survive.

The ensuing battle raged for seeming eons. Many of our race were killed, but the Flatteners fled into the night and stayed away long enough for us to pillage their food stock. We have enough in our silos to last us for many years to come.

We have not yet been able to live above ground again. The Flatteners regrouped and returned. Our land, as we know it, is gone. Although they continue to demolish our anthills, we have constructed so many that the few they destroy don't matter. Besides, the young ones prefer life in our cool, quiet, dark colony. This is where they want to raise our future generations.

We did not rid ourselves of the Flatteners, but we know they can be defeated if necessary. You see, spirit always survives.

They say that blood is thicker than water. Maybe that's why we battle our own with more energy and gusto than we would ever expend on strangers.

David Assael, *Northern Exposure, Family Feud, 1993*

***

Family isn't about whose blood you have. It's about who you care about.

Trey Parker and Matt Stone, *South Park, Ike's Wee Wee, 1998*

MEASURED STEPS

"He's intelligent, mannerly, and gentle, but strong." Giselle spoke in a dreamy tone to Mavis. "He's the best man I've ever met."

"I can tell by the look in your eyes. It's about time you took your nose out of those books and let someone get close to you," Mavis said with a mixture of scolding and relief. She rolled her dark eyes up comically and exhaled dramatically.

"I know I haven't dated in a while."

"A while? You haven't dated since Smokey Robinson left the Miracles," Mavis laughed, tossing her black dreadlocks. "I was ready to have some of the psychiatrists we work with check you out." Mavis poked a well-manicured forefinger into Giselle's temple.

"My standards may be a bit high, but the wait was worth it," Giselle smiled at her best friend.

Giselle Martin was a thirty year old, intelligent, independent, pretty woman. Her golden skin and ebony eyes earned her the admiration of many of the doctors she worked with in her position of Claims Review Manager with at the Henry Behavioral Health Center. Some gave her flowers, some candy. Some were so bold as to put their hands on her five-foot-five slim figure, but soon found that to be a grave error. None could warm her heart.

Most of her spare time was spent reading. Giselle loved novels and spent an unprecedented amount of time in the Newark Public Library scouring the shelves for the latest mysteries. It was in the library she met Tyson.

Tyson was ahead of Giselle at the book checkout desk. A six-foot-two, husky, impeccably dressed figure holding a stack of love stories seemed odd, but intriguing.

"Are you researching love?" Giselle quipped.

Tyson turned and smiled shyly, answering, "No, but if you need help on the subject, I'm your man."

He invited her to coffee at a little café on Halsey Street.

Giselle didn't know if it was the twinkle in his light brown eyes, his smooth chocolate skin, or his dimpled smile that bowled her over, but by the end of the afternoon she knew was he was the one.

Giselle gazed out her office window while she continued her conversation with Mavis. "I know we just met a few days ago, but I feel like I know him already. He just moved into the area from New Brunswick. I'm glad I met him before some beauty queen scoffed him up."

"You just remember you're a queen too," Mavis stated with her usual supportiveness.

Giselle dismissed her with a waved hand. "Our conversations feel comforting, somehow familiar. He always knows the right thing to say."

Mavis lifted one eyebrow. "Just be careful, girl. Saying and doing are two different things."

The days that followed were a romantic blur. Tyson took Giselle to the best restaurants, where they dined on exotic foods and drank champagne.

The First Reserve Restaurant had the best Sunday brunch in the Newark area. Tyson and Giselle were ushered to a table on which waited a crystal vase which held one red rose and one white rose.

The hostess smiled as she sat them and said, "Will there be anything else, sir?"

Tyson waved her off politely.

Giselle asked, "What does she mean anything else? She hasn't given us anything yet." Then she noticed a small, white, embossed card hanging from the vase by a thin gold ribbon. In the finest calligraphy it read, "*Of all things bright and beautiful, nothing can touch one as fair as you. All my love, Tyson "*

Tyson smiled warmly and looked deep into Giselle's eyes. "That's what she means."

The following evening Giselle was settling down to a quiet cup of Chamomile tea and television. The commercial for a new action movie was blaring from the set for the twentieth time that week.

The hero was sitting, bloodied on a rickety wooden chair with his arms tied behind him, head hung low. Giselle rolled her eyes as the villain said, *"This is the end for you."*

The doorbell rang. She opened the door to find Tyson standing on the porch sporting a silly grin.

"What are you so happy about?" Giselle said grinning back at him.

"I have something special for you." Tyson stepped to his left to reveal a large box with holes punched in the top.

"What in the world?" Giselle knelt and removed the lid to reveal a tiny black kitten with a bandage on his front right leg. He was asleep in one corner of the box on a thick white terrycloth towel.

Giselle squealed with delight waking the kitten who began mewing along with her. She lifted him carefully, avoiding the bandaged leg. "What happened to his leg?" Giselle rocked the little black bundle and cooed soothingly.

"The people at the pound said it was brought in with a broken leg. They were going to put him to sleep, but I wanted to rescue him."

"Thank you, Tyson. I love him…and you too." Giselle continued cooing until the kitten quieted. "What shall we call him?"

"How about Buttons, because he's cute as a button?" Tyson said still grinning.

Giselle smiled, "Buttons it is."

Tuesday evening Tyson cooked dinner for Giselle at his two floor townhouse. It was her first visit to his home. While he simmered his red beans and rice specialty and snapped fresh string beans, Giselle wandered from room to room admiring the artwork on his walls.

Tyson collected original artwork, oil paintings, and African masks. His townhouse was like a museum of African art. Giselle knew little about art, but admired his choice of color and style. As she padded her bare feet into the thick carpeted stairs to the second floor, she called down to Tyson, "Can I help with anything?"

Tyson answered, "No, Honey. You just take a look around. I'd like you to become familiar with my place so you'll be comfortable."

There were three closed doors on the second floor.

The first opened to a mauve colored bathroom. It was the largest bathroom Giselle had ever seen. There was a wood paneled hot tub for two in one corner. Huge, soft, burgundy towels trimmed in kenti cloth hung from towel racks near the tub and pedestal sink. Glass encased a mauve and burgundy tiled shower. Shower jets sprouted from the tiles high and low. A small black stool sat in the center of the shower floor. Giselle imagined herself relaxing there as hot jets of water massaged her muscles.

Tyson broke her reverie, "Giselle, dinner will be ready in a few minutes."

Resisting the urge to peek into his medicine cabinet, she quickened her pace to see the rest of the second floor.

The master bedroom was next. It was nothing short of magnificent. Giselle stood in awe in the middle of the deep brown plush carpet. She was somewhat ashamed that her modestly tasteful home couldn't rival

Tyson's.   The room was a rich mixture of bronze and gold.

Rich African tapestries hung from the walls.   An imposing antique ebony dresser displayed small soapstone sculptures at one end and a copper platter of thick, golden, pungent candles on the other.   A matching hand carved mirror hung on the wall over the dresser.

The most outstanding piece in the room was a majestic king sized four poster bed.   It stood in front of a huge picture window framed with heavy gold jacquard drapes, tied back with bronze tassels.   A deep bronze paisley patterned satin down comforter lay across the bed and was decorated with multiple brown and gold pillows.

The room reminded Giselle of stories of harems and Arabian nights.   She envisioned herself stretched out on that bed watching the stars twinkle.

Tyson snatched Giselle from her dreams, "Dinner's ready."   He was standing at the bottom of the stairwell.

"I'll be right there," she called down to him.   On the way to the stairs, Giselle turned the knob of the third door.   It swung open to reveal a room lined with bookshelves on all four walls.   There were books and movies everywhere, tomes, paperbacks, compact discs, as well as, a computer.   A desk sat mid-room.   Each corner of the desk held a neat pile.   One corner had a tall stack of paperback books.   The next, magazines.   The two corners nearest the high back leather chair held the old fashioned traditional black and white notebooks used in primary schools and a wooden tray stuffed with scribbled notes.

Looking down, Giselle noticed what looked like a driver's license on the floor.   She picked it up and scanned it.   The name read Tyler Banks.   *Who's Tyler Banks?*

"Giselle!" Tyson said right at her ear.

Giselle let out a little scream, dropping the license.

Tyson reached in front of her and pulled the door

shut with a bang. In an even, controlled voice Tyson said, "Dinner is on the table, Dear."

After eating, they cuddled before the blazing livingroom fireplace on a soft loveseat and drank cognac. Giselle gushed at how perfect his home was.

"The only thing I don't see are family photos."

"I don't have any," Tyson replied stiffly. "My parents died when I was a child, and I don't have any brothers or sisters. I really don't want to discuss it. Ok?"

"I'm sorry I asked, but if you ever want to talk about it, I'm here." Changing the subject, Giselle continued asking questions about the artwork and commenting on his luscious décor.

"The only room I haven't seen closely is your library. What do you have in there, dead bodies?" Giselle laughed.

Tyson sat up straight, removed his arm from her back and said seriously, "That's a private room."

Startled, Giselle mumbled an apology for asking the question. Tyson relaxed and resumed his loving personae. The evening progressed into deep kisses and more. As she wished, Giselle got to see the stars from Tyson's bedroom window.

Giselle awoke about 3a.m. and stumbled to the bathroom. On her way back to the bed, curiosity overcame her prior apology. She crept to Tyson's library and tried the doorknob. Locked! *I guess he was serious about the privacy thing.* She went back to bed and slept until morning.

Back home late that morning after much snuggling and a hearty breakfast, Giselle fed Buttons kitten food. He made little smacking noises as he ate. Cradling the telephone on one shoulder she told Mavis about the prior evening, making the story just juicy enough to make her salivate without giving too many details.

"He sounds perfect," Mavis sighed. "I'd hold on to him."

"Only one thing…"

"Oh boy, here we go. Every man you meet has something wrong. When are you going to understand that no one's perfect!" Mavis' voice rose.

"But this was strange," Giselle said. She told Mavis about the locked library door.

"I wouldn't worry about that, girl," Mavis said. "Everyone wants some privacy. You know, your own space? Hasn't that been your excuse for years?"

Giselle had to admit she'd used that line about needing more space quite often. By the time the conversation ended, she felt silly for even bringing it up.

Giselle knelt and picked up Buttons. He mewed loudly as if in pain. *I wonder if I need medication for him.* She climbed into her blue Corolla. With Buttons in his brand new cat carrier, they headed to the Humane Society.

Arriving at the pound she carried Buttons to the front desk. A young girl with a bad case of acne was watching a small television. The same action movie commercial that so irritated Giselle seemed to have the girl entranced.

Giselle cleared her throat loudly.

"Miss Pimples" turned and glanced into the cage. "Hey, what happened to him?"

"My boyfriend bought him from here two days ago."

"Yeah, I remember. But what happened to him?" The girl was now peering closely at Buttons.

"What do you mean? He was purchased with this broken leg. I should be asking you what happened to him." Giselle was becoming aggravated. "Is there a manager I can speak to?"

Ignoring Giselle, the pimply girl said, "He didn't leave here like that!" She pointed a skinny finger at Buttons. "A kitten with a broken leg would be put to sleep before any non-employee saw him. We sold this kitten in good health, and I can prove it."

Before Giselle could respond the girl shuffled through a pile of papers in a tray on her desk. "Most people want dogs. The only cats we sold in the past two days are here." Five seconds later she whipped out a wrinkled form. It showed the purchase of a healthy six week old black male kitten. The signature was Tyler Banks.

Giselle left the pound carrying Buttons who sported a brand new cast on his leg. She sat in her Corolla, hands on steering wheel and stared into space. *How did Buttons break his leg, and why wouldn't Tyson tell me what happened?* She tried to dismiss the morbid questions as imagination.

Back home Giselle and Mavis explored the possibilities.

"Girl, you don't know what happened. Buttons could have jumped out of the car. Tyson is probably just ashamed he let the kitten get hurt."

"But he could have admitted it to me. I wouldn't hold it against him."

"Maybe you should concentrate on holding your body against him and forget about Buttons' leg," Mavis laughed.

"What about the name? The form had Tyson's address, but that other guy's name."

"I don't know. Maybe it's a pen name or maybe he had a name change. Maybe this Tyler guy is a friend." Annoyance crept into Mavis' voice. "Ask him. I'm sure he'll have a good explanation."

In a way Mavis made sense, but the nagging questions continued to dance in Giselle's mind.

That Saturday Giselle, Tyson and Buttons went South Mountain Reservation for an afternoon picnic. It was an idyllic day for the outing. The blue sky was spotted with fluffy clouds, and the sun shone brightly without dispensing oppressive heat.

Tyson carried a large wicker basket with one hand and a beautiful African print blanket under his other arm. Giselle held Buttons close to her chest as the kitten clawed at her necklace.

They found a shady spot under a huge maple tree and spread out a lunch of shrimp salad sandwiches, iced tea and chocolate chip cookies. Giselle kept Buttons tied to her wrist with a small expanding leash. He leapt around in the tall grass like a tiny bunny rabbit. Giselle and Tyson spent the afternoon laughing, eating and watching Buttons.

Taking advantage of the relaxed atmosphere Giselle asked, "Tyson, who is Tyler Banks?"

Tyson answered almost before she finished the question, "He was a very close friend of mine. Unfortunately, he passed away a couple of years ago." He looked down at the blanket wistfully. "I saw you looking at his driver's license that night. He lost his wallet at my place. I didn't find it until after he died."

Giselle wanted to ask what happened to Buttons and why he used Tyler's name at the pound, but didn't know how to approach the subject.

Tyson ended any attempts she might have made to continue the conversation, "Giselle, if we're going to be together, you have to trust me. Without trust there can't be a true relationship."

"I trust you, Tyson…and love you."

The following Friday Giselle's boss called her into his office at closing time. "Can't someone else fill in for Mavis this evening? Tonight is special." Giselle rarely complained about extra duties, but Tyson was taking her to The Lakeside Restaurant this evening. It was the most fabulous eatery in the area. She had never been able to afford to go there, and she wasn't going to miss it now.

"Sorry Giselle. No one else is available. I wouldn't ask if it wasn't important." Joe gave her his best sad puppy dog eyes, the ones Giselle couldn't resist. The tiny television he kept on his office credenza buzzed in the background.

"The least you can do is to turn off that annoying movie commercial. I've seen it a hundred times."

Giselle grimaced as the villain said, *"This is the end for you."*

Joe laughed, "Everyone's seen this a hundred times. It's the biggest movie out this year. I can't wait to see it myself." He reached back and clicked off the television. He waited silently for Giselle to acquiesce.

She complied. "The best I can do is to take the files home and work on them over the weekend."

"Thanks!" Joe grinned. "I won't forget this." He made a quick getaway.

Still grimacing, Giselle slid the papers into a brown expanding file, tied the cord, and sat them on the desk next to her handbag.

Later that evening, Giselle excitedly dressed. She had purchased a golden yellow crepe dress with dolman sleeves and a long skirt which fit her to a tee. The neckline dipped just low enough to hint at her cleavage. She wore her hair in a French twist and adorned herself with a pair of gold chandelier earrings which Tyson had given her. Wearing the highest gold heels she could stand, she made a grand entrance from the top of the stairway.

Tyson stood at the bottom of the steps grinning ear to ear as he watched her descend. When she reached him, he took her hand and kissed it fervently. "No woman in existence ascends your beauty."

They drove to the Lakeside Restaurant. It was perfect. Fresh flowers, candlelight, peach colored tablecloths, high back, hand carved wooden chairs with matching peach cushions, live violins and piano music from a far corner of the room.

After a delectable dinner of oysters on the half shell, stuffed lobster tails and champagne, Giselle and Tyson danced to the soft, slow sounds of the violins. Giselle floated across the floor. She was so giddy; she couldn't even remember ordering the meal. They held each other tightly and vowed never to let go.

They returned to their table for one more glass of champagne and dessert. Tyson motioned to the waiter. He walked over with a massive tray of dessert selections and presented it to Giselle. Centered in the tray was a small gold box tied with a gold ribbon.

"What's that?" Giselle quizzed, still glowing from her dance.

"This is a special dessert for you, Madame." The maitre'd bowed his head.

Shaking with anticipation, Giselle reached for the box. She looked at Tyson, who shrugged. She quickly pulled the bow loose and lifted the box top. Inside was the most beautiful diamond ring she had ever seen. She gasped as Tyson picked up the ring and got down on one knee.

The restaurant hushed. Tyson took Giselle's shaking hand and said, "Giselle, you are the only one who speaks to my heart. Accept this ring and intertwine our souls forever. Marry me."

Giselle responded the only way possible, "Yes."

That evening they made love like it was the first time. They barely closed Giselle's door when Tyson kissed her fervently. He crushed her against the door and ran his hands over her sleek body, stopping only to cup her round bottom and pull her even closer.

Giselle moaned softly as her heart quickened. She began to unbutton his shirt, but in her heat ripped it open. Buttons pattered to the foyer floor.

Tyson lifted Giselle in his muscular arms and carried her upstairs to the bedroom. He stood her in front of the bed. Giselle opened her mouth to speak.

"Shhh. Don't say a word." Tyson whispered. He reached around her body and slowly unzipped her dress. Pulling it down over her bosom, he let it drop to the floor, leaving her only in black lace thongs. He laid Giselle back on the thick down comforter and quickly undressed.

Again, he crushed her with his heated body. He kissed her face, eyelids, mouth; licked her ears; sucked her neck, then her erect nipples.

Giselle could no longer remain silent. She cried out, "Tyson, Tyson!" She scratched at his back as he nipped and bit at her soft belly.

Suddenly, he reached down and ripped her thongs from her thighs. Giselle screamed, "Please, Tyson, I can't wait! I need you now!"

Tyson gave her all she desired.

The next morning Giselle awoke to find a deep red rose on Tyson's pillow. Attached was a note. *Last night the universe stood in awe of us. Love, Tyson.*

Giselle sighed. *He always knows the perfect thing to say.*

After a long, hot shower, Giselle began picking up her strewn clothing. In the folds of her heavy bronze and ivory comforter she found one gold earring. She shook out the tangled bedding and searched fervently under the bed for the other earring with no luck. Giselle backtracked through the events of the evening.

After thoroughly searching the house, she finally concluded the only possibilities…Tyson's car or the restaurant. Giselle called Tyson's home and cell phone – no answer. *I might as well check the restaurant.*

Later that afternoon Giselle walked into the Lakeside and asked for the maitre-d. He recognized her from the previous evening. "Miss Giselle, did you enjoy your evening last night?"

"How did you know my name?"

"Your gentleman planned the evening well in advance. He took a copy of the menu and compared it to a novel he brought with him."

"A novel?"

The maitre-d bowed his head elegantly and smiled, "Yes, I believe it was called "Windy roses". There was a chapter which included a romantic dinner. He asked us to prepare the exact meal."

Giselle stood silent, absorbing this revelation.

The maitre-d continued in his smooth voice, "He thinks very highly of you to go through such trouble. But please excuse me Miss. How can I help you today?"

Giselle mumbled distractedly, "I lost an earring. Did anyone find it?"

"I'll check Miss." He smoothed his way down the hall.

As she waited, Giselle rethought the evening. *No wonder I didn't remember ordering the meal. It was already planned.*

"Sorry, Miss. No one turned in an earring. If we find it, how may we contact…"

Giselle turned and walked out without answering.

Giselle entered the Barnes and Noble bookstore on route 10. The East Hanover store was large and sure to have what she needed. The clerk assured her they had "Windy roses" in the romance section. Sure enough it was exactly where the clerk indicated. It was a paperback with a black cover showing blood red roses blowing in the wind, naturally.

As Giselle stood in line to pay, she despairingly spied a large poster touting the book from which the new action movie was produced. It showed the villain leaning back, arms outstretched, smoke steaming upward from his mouth, his bright red jacket flapping in the breeze. Beneath him was the quote *"This is the end for you."*

Giselle quickly retrieved the book and returned home.

Upon entering her home, Giselle plopped down on the couch to scan the book, when she remembered the paperwork she promised to process over the weekend. *"Roses" can wait.* She tossed the book on the couch and started to her home office.

The telephone rang. Giselle answered to find an excited Mavis on the other end.

"So, how was your evening?" Mavis' grin could be heard through the line.

"It was wonderful," Giselle said distractedly. "What color would you like to wear?"

"What do you mean?"

"As my maid of honor," Giselle paused to let Mavis absorb the information.

Mavis squealed so loudly Giselle almost dropped the receiver.

Giselle described the evening in dreamy tones. She felt her doubts melting away as she shared the news with her friend.

"Now Mavis, don't get mad," Giselle said cautiously. "I just want your opinion."

"On what?"

Giselle repeated her conversation with the maitred.

Mavis said, "I think that's so thoughtful. He wanted everything to be perfect."

Giselle hesitated, then replied, "That's what I thought too. Thanks Mavis."

Giselle ascended the stairs to her extra bedroom which she used as an office. It was equipped with a desk, computer, printer, scanner and such, as well as, a telephone. She opened the expanding file and pulled out the manila folders. The patients' names were written on the folder tabs. Their diagnoses were written across the top of the folder.

Giselle was to review each file to ensure complete information was entered. If not, she would follow up with the patients or doctors by phone and fill in the missing data. Psychiatric patients had to be handled delicately. Joe liked the calm, smooth voice Giselle used to speak to the clients. When she assured them of confidentiality, they believed her with no qualms.

Giselle quickly scanned the first few files without finding omissions. She picked up the next folder and froze. The name on the tab was Tyler Banks! *Isn't that the name I found at Tyson's?* The words "Undiagnosed Personality Disorder" were written on the folder front. The folder was thick with paperwork dating back twenty years.

Giselle turned to the back of the folder and started with the oldest form. As a child, Tyler had a history of hurting small animals. At the tender age of ten he cut off his neighbor's dog's tail. Later his parents found what they assumed to be road kill in his bedroom in a cooler. It was never determined if Tyler killed them or found them dead.

Tyler had various social problems growing up, mostly based on an inability to fit into his peer groups. In his teens he graduated from cutting animals to cutting people. The older he became the more antisocial he became. He held several low paying jobs for short periods of time. He was eventually institutionalized in Marlboro State Hospital. After two years of intensive therapy, Tyler was released as a person able to assimilate into society.

As a condition of his release, Tyler was required to make outpatient visits to the Henry Behavioral Health Center twice yearly. In one of his sessions, he revealed that he first learned to act like normal people by imitating what he saw on the hospital television. When he was released from Marlboro, he continued this educational route, adding movies and books to his studies.

In subsequent sessions he told the psychiatrists he no longer made a move without first consulting a book, magazine, or movie. His wardrobe was composed from outfits shown in Gentlemen's Quarterly. The meals he prepared, the car he drove, even the sentences he used were from media sources.

One doctor noted Tyler seemed proud he had finally achieved normalcy by society's standards, even if it was false normalcy.

Giselle turned over the final review form. It noted his last visit as two weeks ago. *Tyson said he died two years ago!* Giselle shivered. *I'm letting my imagination run away with me. I hope.*

Stapled inside the folder front was the patient's basic information, address, physical description, and such. Tyler lived in New Brunswick. *That's where Tyson lived. I guess that's how they knew each other.* Physical description: six foot two, brown eyes, black hair. *That sounds like Tyson, but it sounds like millions of other men too.* Birth date: October 13, 1970. *It is Tyson!*

She slapped the folder closed. After reading twenty years of history, she had more questions than answers.

A half an hour later Giselle slinked into Staples in West Orange. She wore a New Jersey Bears' baseball cap pulled low over her eyes. Clutching the Tyler Banks folder to her chest, Giselle went to the copy machines. She committed the cardinal sin of making copies of a client's personal file. She had no idea what she would do with the information, but felt compelled to have it.

Back home Giselle tried to calm herself. She brewed a pot of chamomile tea, added honey, and curled up on the couch with the steaming mug. Reaching for the television remote, Giselle spotted the book she'd purchased earlier that day.

She curled the paperback and fanned the pages slowly, looking for the dinner menu she'd so enjoyably consumed. About halfway through the book she found a scene in which the loving couple was having a romantic dinner. As stated by the maitre-d, their exact menu, right down to the Moet champagne was spelled out in black and white. Giselle continued reading. This restaurant also had candles and violins. Giselle's hands tightened as she continued. Two pages later the words "Marry me." seemed to leap from the print. Giselle held the page open and read, "Miriam, you are the only one who speaks to my heart. Accept this ring and intertwine our souls forever. Marry me." Giselle's hands shook as trepidation grew in her heart. She lost her place, reopened the book to the front and started flipping pages rapidly.

The name "Buttons" appeared before her eyes. The page described how the young man presented his future wife with the gift of a tiny black kitten with a broken leg! He said, "Why don't we name him Buttons, because he's cute as a button?"

Giselle dropped the book in horror. Chamomile wouldn't smooth this over.

That evening Tyson convinced Giselle to go see the dreaded action thriller. "I can't wait to see it. I heard the special effects and fight scenes are great! Besides, there's a heroine in the movie. You'll like it."

Giselle never heard Tyson express such enthusiasm for anything before, so she gave in.

The theater was predictably packed, but they had arrived early enough to get good seats. As was her habit, Giselle had smuggled in some grapes for a snack. Tyson settled back and put his arm snugly around her shoulders.

She flinched.   He was grinning like a Cheshire cat. Giselle just tried to hide her mixed nervousness and irritation. For the first time since she met him, Giselle did not want to be in Tyson's presence.

The film turned out to be as exciting as touted. For a couple of hours Giselle forgot her anxieties and became engrossed in the screen. She held her breath at the climax of the movie.

The villain sucked on his slim, chocolate brown cigar, then opened his mouth and pulled the grey smoke up into his nose. The hero was sitting, bloodied on a rickety wooden chair with his arms tied behind him, head hung low. The villain said, "This is the end for you." He stretched out his arms and leaned back laughing heartily as smoke drifted toward the ceiling. His bright red jacket flapped in the breeze of an overhead fan. The beautiful heroine snatched up a rusty pipe and slammed it into the villain's stomach, causing him to double over. She finished the job by hitting him in the back of the head with such force as to split his skull open. Then she woke her hero and untied him. As they looked down on the fallen villain, the heroine stated, "It was either him or us, and we're what matter." She helped him up and they walked into the sunset with him leaning on her shoulders for support.

As they left the theater, Tyson asked, "Would you save me like that?"

Giselle stumbled, "Of course, I would." But she moved out of his reach and walked to the car.

Late Sunday morning Giselle drove down NJ-18 deep in thought. *I don't know what I'll find, but I have to silence my fears.* Following her Mapquest directions she rounded the off ramp onto New Street.

She started with Tyler's last noted job. The Brown Apple Pub was known as much for it's quaint atmosphere as for its weekend brawls. The locals would gather there to drink foreign ales and discuss politics. Mostly on weekends, when the most ale was consumed, the debates would become fist fights. Tyler worked there for about two months, before joining in one of the fights and getting fired.

Giselle entered the dimly lit, smoky tavern at noon. A few tables centered the room, flanked on two sides by booths and a long wooden bar along one wall. Several elbow-benders sat at the bar. A sleazy looking bartender with greasy gray hair pulled back in a ponytail was leaning close to one patron, listening intently to his opinions. A large television hung caddy cornered near the bar showing the never-ending action movie commercial.

"Excuse me," Giselle almost whispered.

Everyone in the bar looked up.

Embarrassed, Giselle walked to the bartender and said, "I'm a reporter writing a story about how employers handle difficult employees. I was told the manager here could help me."

The bartender gave her a man's slow appraising glance, then said, "I'm the manager. Call me Pete."

Annoyed, Giselle replied, "Did you manage an employee named Tyler Banks?"

"Yeah. Why don't we have a drink while we talk?" Pete grinned.

"No thank you. This will be quick."

Pete's mood changed abruptly. "What about him? I'm busy here." He jerked his head toward the patrons who had returned to their own conversations.

"How long did Tyler work for you?" Giselle asked as sweetly as possible.

"A couple of months. He just stocked the back room and the bar, and swept the floors."

"Why did you let him go?"

"He couldn't talk to anyone without getting into a

fight. If we left him alone, he was ok, but conversations set him off." Pete nodded in response to a waved finger. He reached behind him for a bottle of Wild Turkey and started to walk away.

"Wait!" Giselle practically shouted.

Pete turned and said nastily, "Why don't you just go see his family two blocks over. He pointed west. It's the large gray house on the corner." He strode away to service his customer.

She pulled up in front of an old Victorian house. The gray color suited the dilapidated state of the building. The lawn was overgrown and trash littered the porch. The only signs of inhabitation were yellow curtains hanging in the first floor windows.

Giselle walked up the rickety steps and rang the doorbell. The door creaked open two inches, and an old woman with matted gray hair peeped through the crack.

"Yeah?" she croaked.

"Hello. My name is Giselle. I'm looking for Tyler Banks," Giselle asked tentatively.

"Who? Oh, he used to live here. This is my place now." The old lady peered closer at Giselle, then closed the door swiftly. She jangled the door chain and reopened the door. "Come in."

Giselle entered the dark foyer. The house looked as dismal on the inside as out. As she ushered Giselle into the livingroom, the woman seemed to become more ancient with each passing moment. Giselle sat on a threadbare moss green loveseat, while the woman sat in a large flowered armchair baring scratched carved wooden legs and armrests.

"So what do you want to know?" The woman coughed violently and spat into a torn white hankie.

Submerging the urge to gag Giselle asked, "Are you related to Tyler?"

"No. I'm Irma Sling. I've been living here for

some time now." Cough, spit. "I remember him though. He was a good looking boy, tall and handsome, but a hell raiser." Irma looked away thoughtfully, "They say my memory is no good, but I beg to differ. All old people aren't crazy you know."

"Of course not. What can you tell me about Tyler?"

"He was a trouble maker, that one, in and out of jail and the crazy house. He was *young* and crazy!" Cough, spit. "And they call old people crazy." Irma looked dreamily at the ceiling and started humming seemingly random notes.

Giselle was beginning to wonder if she'd get any useful information from Irma. "Does anyone else live here with you who might remember Tyler?"

Irma stopped humming mid-note and looked at Giselle as if seeing her for the first time. "How are you young lady? I'm Irma. It's nice to meet you."

Discouraged, Giselle rose and started to the door.

Irma toddled after her. "Where are you going?"

At the front door Giselle put a hand on Irma's shoulder and said, "Thank you for your time, Irma. It was nice meeting you."

As she opened the door and started to leave, Irma brightened, "The other two were nice, not like Tyler."

Giselle spun around to face Irma. "What other two?"

"His brother and cousin lived here too. You didn't ask about them. His cousin was such a sweet girl. I think her name was Mary or Margaret or something like that."

Excitedly Giselle asked, "Do you know where I can find them?"

Irma kept talking as if she didn't hear Giselle, "Mavis! Yes, that's her name, Mavis."

Giselle fell back against the porch banister, almost toppling into the weeds. She questioned Irma another half hour without getting one coherent sentence from her. Finally giving up, she urged Irma back inside, shut the door and left.

Driving back up the turnpike, Giselle's mind raced. Mavis, her only confidante could no longer be trusted. *She knew Tyson was really Tyler Banks and she urged on the relationship. Why? I can't trust her now.*

That evening Tyson was preparing another of his gourmet meals. Giselle fidgeted nervously on the couch while Tyson chatted animatedly from the kitchen.

"You know, Honey, I was wondering where you'd like to go for our honeymoon? I was thinking of Tahiti."

"I can't think that far ahead, Tyson," Giselle said quietly.

"What did you say, Babe?" Tyson yelled from the kitchen.

"I said I'm going to lie down until dinner is ready."

"Ok. I'll call you when it's ready."

Giselle headed up the stairs looking over her shoulder to be sure Tyson wasn't following her. She went into the bedroom and yanked back the thick coverlet, then punched the pillow, leaving a deep valley in the center.

Turning, she eyed the top of the huge dresser. *Now where would he keep it?* Quietly she opened drawers one by one and stealthily ran her hands through the contents. Finally at the back of the sixth drawer she struck gold. A round gold key ring bearing the picture of an official looking building and the phrase "I love New Brunswick". Two silver keys hung from the ring, one large, one small.

Giselle peeked out the bedroom door, then tiptoed to Tyson's library. It was predictably locked. Listening for footsteps, she fumbled with the larger key. It fit neatly into the lock and turned with a soft click. Giselle easily turned the doorknob and pushed the door open slightly.

From the bottom of the stairs she heard footsteps. She closed the door as quietly as possible and tiptoed back to the bedroom. She was about to lie across the bed when Tyson entered.

"Honey, dinner is ready."

Giselle spun around to face a smiling Tyson. She tightly held the keys of opportunity in her fist. "Hi, Baby. I just got up."

Tyson glanced at the bed. "Don't worry about straightening the comforter. We'll be back up here right after dinner." he chuckled, displaying deep dimples which were once endearing, but now were chilling.

After a dinner of lobster ravioli with grilled shrimp, followed by Tyson's home made sweet potato pie, they indeed retired to the bedroom.

Tyson placed a silver tray with a decanter of cognac and two small stemmed glasses on the nightstand. Giselle and Tyson slowly undressed as candles flickered light over their bodies and filled the room with soothing fragrance. They lay side by side listening to the rhythms of Frankie Beverly and Maze playing softly in the background.

Tyson pulled Giselle close to his warm chest and enfolded her body in his strong arms. His fingers traced lightly down her back to the beginning of her supple buttocks.

Giselle shivered. *No I can't. I want to, but I can't make love to you. I can't love you. I do love you so. Don't touch me there. Please don't kiss me so deeply. Don't make my back rise, my heart thump, my breath shorten, my body sweat, my sex wet. Don't make me respond to you. Don't stop.*

Giselle awakened with a start. The antique clock on the bedside table read two o'clock. Tyson snored contentedly with one arm flung across his face. Quietly,

Giselle slipped out of bed and searched the dark floor for her slacks. Finding them she stuck her hand into the front pocket and found the treasured keys.

Giselle tiptoed to the library after closing the bedroom door. She opened the library door, stepped inside and closed the door behind her. The room was bathed in moonlight from the large windows at the back of the room. Giselle's agenda was clear in her mind. She went to the desk and turned on Tyson's computer. She had been careful to turn off the speakers before booting the computer, but was not prepared for the bright light of the monitor. She flinched as the screen lit up in a bright blue.

Giselle began to explore his files. She found a large file named Reference. A double click of the folder exposed subfolders named Romance, Menus, Love Songs, Fashion, and Décor. Each subfolder contained a list of book and movie titles. It was his library reference! This may be the key to Tyson's past.

Giselle searched Tyson's desk drawers and found blank computer disks. She was copying the Reference file when she heard a muffled sound.

"Giselle, Honey, where are you?"

Giselle went to the library door and called out, "In the bathroom. The shrimp upset my stomach. I'll be there in a minute."

"Do you want me to get you some Pepto-Bismol?"

"No. I'll be right there."

"Ok Sweetie. Hurry back."

Giselle ran to the computer. The file had just finished copying. She turned off the computer and peeped out the library door. All was quiet.

As she slipped back into bed, Tyson quipped sleepily, "You stay in this bed with me. You know I don't trust you as far as I can throw you." He smiled dreamily and went back to sleep.

Back home the next morning Giselle called the health center, "Joe, I'm really sick. I need to stay off my feet for a few days."

"Ok, but I need the files you took home." Joe hesitated then said, "I'll send Mavis by to pick them up. It's only fair since you filled in for her."

The thought of seeing Mavis sent shivers of disgust through Giselle's bones, but she had no choice.

A half hour later Mavis rang Giselle's doorbell. "Hey girl, I hear you're under the weather."

Giselle used her best sick voice, "Yeah. I need to stay in bed a few days."

"Alone?" Mavis grinned.

"Yes, alone!" Giselle snapped.

Mavis frowned, "What's wrong? I thought you two were getting along great."

"We are. I just don't feel well. Here are the files." Giselle handed the expanding file through the doorway to Mavis.

Mavis untied the string and looked inside. "What's so urgent about these files anyway?" She flipped through the files and suddenly froze. A fear flickered in her eyes. "Did you review these files, Giselle?" Mavis asked quietly.

"Yes. I reviewed them thoroughly," she replied watching Mavis' reaction closely. "What's the matter Mavis? Is there something in those files you didn't want me to see?"

Mavis cautiously pulled her gaze from the files to Giselle's eyes. Fear met anger.

"Why didn't you tell me about Tyson?" Giselle asked in a controlled voice.

Still playing dumb, Mavis replied, "What about him?"

"That he's your cousin for one thing!"

"How did you know that?"

"Just answer me. How could you approve the relationship when you knew all about him?"

"He just needs a little help. You're good for him. He really cares about you," Mavis pleaded.

"A little help?" Giselle yelled. "He's psychotic!"

"No he's not," Mavis averred. "He has his little quirks like anyone else. He just wants to please you."

"I read his records. He's nuts. Not only nuts, he's dangerous." Giselle crossed her arms tightly across her chest.

"What records?"

Giselle reached into the expanding file and grabbed Tyler's folder. "These records."

"This isn't Tyson's file. It's his brother Tyler's"

Giselle's eyes popped. "His brother? Then why do they have the same birth date?"

"They're twins," Mavis said like it was the most obvious answer in the world.

Giselle stood in silent absorption for a second. Then calmly she said, "We'd better sit down."

The next hour and a half were the most compelling in Giselle's life.

"So, you mean to tell me Tyson is normal?"

"Well, pretty much. He was heavily influenced by Tyler's psychotic nature. He wanted to separate himself from his brother's violent acts. They were fraternal twins, so there was little resemblance, and he changed his name to Brooke so people wouldn't make a connection. I've been their guardian since the death of my aunt and uncle. They were found stabbed multiple times. My uncle was dead when the police arrived. My aunt was unconscious. At the hospital she opened her eyes just long enough to make me promise to care for the boys. Then she died. I kept that promise.

Their parents left them a hefty inheritance which was kept in trust. Tyson received all his money on his eighteenth birthday, but the will stipulated that Tyler be doled out a monthly allowance, just enough to sustain him. My aunt and uncle were afraid Tyler's destructiveness would grow uncontrollably if he had wealth.

Since they were dead, and I gave up guardianship when they turned eighteen, Tyson dispensed Tyler's allowance to him."

"For years after his parents' death Tyson reverted into a quiet shell. He wouldn't date girls or even hang out with the guys. Remarkably, both he and Tyler found the same solution for their social ineptness."

Giselle leaned forward. "You mean they both copied their personalities from books and movies?"

Mavis nodded, "I guess that twin synergy was working. As much as Tyson wanted to be different from his brother, he still thought like him in some ways."

Giselle felt her tensions easing. "Now that I think about it, when I asked questions in New Brunswick, I only asked about Tyler. I never mentioned Tyson's name. I was so convinced they were the same person."

Mavis jumped up and grabbed Giselle by the shoulders. "What do you mean New Brunswick? Were you asking around about Tyler?"

"Yeah, but it doesn't matter now that I know Tyson is ok."

"That's not the point! Tyler is very violent. If he finds out you were asking about him, he'll come looking for you. Listen, Giselle, I haven't told you everything."

"There's more?" Giselle asked exasperatedly.

"I was elated when the boys reached their eighteenth birthdays, because I could legally be free of Tyler. He's crazy and dangerous. He threatened me more than once. I had times when I feared for my life. If I hadn't made a death-bed promise to my aunt to care for the twins, I would have abandoned Tyler long ago. As a matter of fact both Tyson and I cut all communications with

Tyler. He doesn't even know where we live. Tyson arranged for an attorney to dole out Tyler's monthly allowance."

Hesitantly, Giselle asked, "Did Tyler have anything to do with the death of his parents?"

Mavis breathed a deep sigh. "I don't know. The police questioned him, but found no evidence pointing to him."

"But in your heart how do you feel?" Giselle held her breath.

"I don't think about it anymore. It's too horrible to imagine."

"Well, I'm not going back down there. Maybe he'll never know. And speaking of not knowing, don't you dare tell Tyson I was checking up on him. I want to be his wife more than ever now."

"He won't hear it from me." Mavis rose to leave. At the door she turned to Giselle and said, "I can't wait until were really cousins."

Their hug contracted the secret between them.

Comforted by the conversation, Giselle settled down in her bed and clicked on the television. *I might as well make a mini vacation out of these few days off.*

The news anchor had just finished up the world events and was beginning the local news. "A tragic discovery this morning in New Brunswick. Eighty two year old Irma Sling was found this morning by her home health aide. She had been knifed to death by an unknown assailant." They changed to a live picture of Irma's home surrounded by police cars, lights flashing.

Giselle held the remote, frozen mid air. Her thumping heart drowned out the rest of the newscaster's words.

Giselle grabbed the telephone and dialed Mavis at the health center. An automated voice answered, "You have reached the desk of blah, blah, blah."

Giselle left a message, "Mavis, call me. It's urgent!" The vacation was over.

Giselle pace the house anxiously. *Should I call the police? What would I tell them anyway? Should I tell Tyson? I can't risk losing him.* The telephone rang abruptly, jolting Giselle from her thoughts.

"Mavis?"

Tyson's deep, mellow voice said, "No, Honey, it's me."

"H-h-hey Baby."

"What's the matter? You sound strange," Tyson asked concerned.

"Nothing's wrong, Honey. I was just expecting a call from Mavis."

"Oh. I just called to see what you needed, cold medicine, tissues…or *anything else*," Tyson smiled through the telephone line.

"No thanks, Baby. I'm fine. I just need to rest, you know, sleep." Giselle put emphasis on the word 'sleep' hoping Tyson would get the message.

"Ok, Sweetie, I'll call later. Love you."

"I love you too, Tyson." Giselle hoped desperation didn't show in her voice. She hung up the phone and lay down to await Mavis' call.

The phone jangled almost immediately. "What's up, girl?" Mavis said worriedly. "You sounded upset."

Giselle related the news report to Mavis.

Mavis whispered, "You should go to the police right now."

"I don't want Tyson to find out I was checking on him. Besides Irma wasn't all there, if you know what I mean. She probably didn't even remember me."

"She remembered me, Tyson and Tyler from years ago, so she remembered you."

"I was probably the last person to see Irma alive. Suppose the police try to pin the murder on me," Giselle practically squealed.

"Are you crazy? Your life is in danger! If Tyler got your name, he'll find you."

"I guess it's only a matter of time before the police question me anyway. The bartender is sure to remember me. Ok, I'll call the police."

Still unsure if this was the right action to take, Giselle made the instinctive move to drive to Penn Station in Newark and use a phone booth there. She dialed nervously and was put through to the detective handling Irma's case.

"Detective Chilly here," the gruff voice answered.

"I believe I have information regarding the Irma Sling case."

"Let's hear it, Honey."

Without giving her name, Giselle quickly explained why she thought Tyler was the killer.

Chilly listened patiently, then replied, "Ma'am how did you come by this information?"

Giselle hesitated at the unexpected question.

Chilly continued, "The reason I ask is because the last known person to see Ms Sling was a young woman. You wouldn't happen to be that woman, would you?"

Giselle slammed down the receiver and stood shaking, feeling alone and scared.

A half hour later, Giselle approached her home. As she drove toward her driveway, she noticed an unfamiliar man partially hidden behind the fir tree in her front yard, peeping into her livingroom window. She slowed to observe him more closely. He was tall and thin with a gaunt face, and neat appearance. As he raised his hands to the sides of his head and leaned closer to the window, Giselle noticed a black blotch spanning the back of his right hand. She sped up and drove to Mavis' apartment.

Giselle was standing at Mavis' front door when she arrived home a little after six o'clock. Once inside,

Giselle related her conversation with Detective Chilly. Then she described the man seen peeking into her window. "He was tall, skinny and sickly looking."

"That sounds like Tyler alright." Mavis furrowed her forehead. "And maybe calling the police wasn't a good idea. Are you sure you clearly explained the situation?"

"Yes. But his immediate reaction was to question my motives. The police are the least of my worries. My biggest fear is Tyler."

"He has tracked you down. I don't want you to go back home."

"You don't have to worry about that, but what about Tyson? He's going to wonder why I'm not home."

"Can't you stay with him a while? I'm sure he wouldn't object." Mavis would have grinned if the situation wasn't so grim.

Tyson readily agreed to Giselle's request for refuge. "I'm just tired of looking at my four walls. Staying at your place a while would be like having a mini vacation. Besides, I'd get to eat more of that good cooking," Giselle smiled masking her troubled thoughts.

Tyson replied eagerly, "Baby, you can stay as long as you like. You can sell your house and move in for all I care."

Mavis drove Giselle to the street which ran parallel to her own. Giselle walked through her neighbor's yard and climbed the short chicken wire fence which divided their back yards. She entered her home through the back door and bolted it securely behind her. Without turning on any lights she quickly packed Buttons and some essentials, and returned to Mavis the way she had come.

As she returned Giselle to her Toyota, Mavis apologized, "Giselle, I'm so sorry about this."

"It isn't your fault, I went nosing around."

"But if I had told you about Tyson and Tyler earlier. This wouldn't have happened. I just wanted you to get to know Tyson before making any judgments."

"I understand, Mavis, and I'm very happy with Tyson. You're still my most precious friend."

Tyson received Giselle with a warm hug. "Hi Honey. Dinner is on the stove." After settling in, Giselle tried to relax on Tyson's plush livingroom sofa. She had brought her copy of 'Windy roses'. With feet up she perused the pages while the fireplace roared.

Tyson approached Giselle and said, "Dinner's almost ready…"

Giselle looked up to see Tyson staring openmouthed at her paperback. Immediately Giselle understood the look. *How stupid can I be?*

Tyson stuttered, "I-it's a good book. I've read it."

Awkwardly Giselle answered, "I just started it. I don't usually read love stories, but it was recommended to me." She stood up, threw the book down on the couch and said, "I'll help you set the table."

They enjoyed a delicious dinner of grilled salmon, whipped sweet potatoes, Caesar salad and cornbread, complimented by a wonderful chardonnay. They completed the meal by spooning fresh strawberries onto mounds of French vanilla ice cream and feeding each other. The remaining evening hours melted into cognac and smooth jazz by the fireplace.

Giselle fell asleep on the shag rug with Buttons cuddled at her feet in front of the blazing fire. Tyson picked her up and carried her to the bed. He laid her there gently and allowed her to sleep through the night.

When she awoke the next morning, Tyson was still sleeping deeply. Giselle carried a light breakfast of toast and tea on a silver tray into the livingroom. She sat on the couch and looked around for her novel. After making a thorough search, she gave up and ate her meal.

Tyson padded down the stairs to the livingroom.

"Hi Sweetie," he yawned. "How'd you sleep?"

"Like a baby…that is like *your* baby."

They smiled.

As Tyson started back up the stairs, Giselle asked, "Honey, did you see my book? I left it on the couch yesterday."

Tyson stopped mid-step. Without turning to face her he said, "No, Honey, I didn't."

"Tyson, let's talk," Giselle said reluctantly.

He turned toward her and replied, "No good conversation starts that way." He returned to the livingroom and sat next to Giselle.

She took his large hands in her delicate ones and said, "Tyson, I know you used that book as a guide for our engagement night."

Tyson's shoulders slumped. He hung his head.

Giselle continued, "Its ok. I'm flattered you thought enough of me to make that night perfect."

Tyson looked hopeful. "Really?"

"Absolutely. You're a wonderful man, and I can't wait to marry you, but there's one thing you must do."

"What's that?" Tyson asked cautiously.

"Be yourself. I want to know the man I marry is a genuine person, not a concoction of book characters."

"You may not like the real me. I don't even know how to be just me."

"We can explore the real you together. Ok?"

The kissed on the deal.

Tyson pulled her up from the couch and began leading her to the bedroom when Giselle stopped him.

"I have to ask one more thing."

Tyson tilted his head, "Yes?"

"What happened to Buttons' leg?"

Tyson sighed, "He jumped out of the car window while I was driving. We were almost at your door, and he didn't seem too hurt, so I tied his leg with a handkerchief."

Giselle sighed relief, grabbed Tyson's hand and pulled him up the stairs.

That afternoon while Tyson was at work, Giselle met Mavis for lunch at a little café a few blocks from the health center. It had a charming atmosphere and was located across from Military Park. As usual, they sat near the front cafe window so they could watch the passersby, especially good looking guys.

They spoke in hushed voices.

"I think you should take a leave of absence and stay with Tyson as long as possible," Mavis offered. "Give Tyler a chance to cool off."

"Give up my job and apartment?" Giselle asked exasperatedly.

"Are they so great that you'd give your life for them?"

"Maybe you're right. Tyson said I could move in if I wanted to."

Mavis squealed, "Really?"

Giselle couldn't hold back the smile, "Yeah, really."

"So you and my cousin are doing well." Mavis' face split into a bright grin. "I guess our days of guy watching are over."

"We're growing closer by the minute." Giselle looked out the window wistfully; then squinted her eyes.

"Hey. Didn't you hear what I just said about guy watching?"

"Shhh!" Giselle covered her face with her menu. "That's the guy that was at my house!" Giselle pointed at a park bench across the street.

Mavis turned too late. "Where?"

Giselle lowered her shield. "He's gone," she said with dismay.

"But how would he know we were here?"

"I'm telling you it was that man."

"Ok. I believe you. Did he see us?"

"I have no idea. Let's get out of here."

After quick goodbyes, they slipped out of the rear exit of the café.

Safe in Tyson's kitchen, Giselle scourged the cabinets and found some chamomile tea. Taking her steaming treasure up to the bedroom she thought again about Tyson's library. *Maybe there's something in the computer files about Tyler.*

Giselle retrieved the key and entered the library. In the daylight it looked more normal. She turned on the computer and waited for it to warm up. As she waited she looked down at the key ring. *What's the small key for?*

Giselle glanced around the room for a safe or lock box. Seeing nothing, she pulled at a desk drawer. It was locked. She slipped the key into a lock on the center drawer. It fit perfectly. She was then able to open all the desk drawers.

In the bottom left hand drawer she found hanging files as neatly arranged as Tyson's desk top. Each file held a neatly labeled manila envelope. The files names read finance, recipes, taxes, and so on. Giselle saw nothing was out of the ordinary, until she reached the last envelope. It was simply marked "T.B.".

Giselle sat in the high backed chair and opened the envelope. There was a photo of a young Tyson standing with his arm around the shoulders of another boy. The other boy was slim and gangly with large hands. Giselle flipped the photo over and read "Tyson and Tyler, 1980". Taking a magnifying glass from the center drawer, Giselle looked more closely at the boys and gasped. Tyler had a black mark on the back of one hand!

The magnifying glass crashed to the floor shattering into glistening shards. In the following silence, Giselle heard the BMW motor of Tyson's car. She

quickly dropped to her knees and scooped the glass frag-
ments into her hands. Little blood dots covered her palms
as she dropped the shiny bits into her pants pockets. Hast-
ily she turned off the computer, returned the "T.B." file
and relocked the desk. She could hear Tyson enter the
foyer and approach the bottom of the stairwell. Giselle
ran into the bathroom to flush the glass and wash the
blood off her hands just as Tyson reached the top of the
stairs.

Tyson knocked on the bathroom door. "I'm home,
Honey," he grinned.

Giselle came out of the bathroom wiping her hands
on a burgundy guest towel. "What did you say?"

"I said 'I just love coming home to you." Tyson
gave her the bear hug she had come to love.

About midnight Tyson and Giselle were awakened
by the doorbell. Tyson donned his robe and went down
the stairs. Giselle stayed atop the stairs straining to understand the muffled voices until she heard a deep moan ema-
nate from Tyson's throat. She ran down to the foyer to
find two police officers holding Tyson up from either side.

"What happened? What's wrong?" Giselle ran to
Tyson's side as they sat him on the couch.

Tyson sobbed, "I can't believe it. My cousin's
dead."

Giselle's throat tightened, "Your cousin?"

"My cousin, Mavis." Tyson buried his head into
Giselle's bosom.

The officers walked to the door. As they left, one
turned and said, "We're sorry for your loss sir."

Giselle's voice hitched. "What happened?"

"They said she was found stabbed outside her
apartment. In her address book she had noted me as her
the person to notify in case of an accident."

Tyson held Giselle in a desperate grip. "She was
my only relative. She was like a mother to me."

Giselle wrapped her arms around him. "I know, Baby. She practically raised you."

Tyson stopped crying abruptly and sat straight up. "How do you know she raised me?"

"Baby, we should talk about this later, when you're not so upset."

Tyson's voice deepened and steadied, "Let's talk about it now."

She could have told him anything, but she told the truth, the whole truth; the medical records; breaking into his library; New Brunswick; Irma Sling; and seeing Tyler.

Tyson listened in silence. When Giselle finished, he stood up and said evenly, "I want you to leave...now."

"L-leave? Didn't you hear what I said?" Giselle's astonished face had no effect on Tyson.

"I heard every word. While I was loving you, you've been sneaking behind my back checking up on me. I took you into my home, and you went into my private records to see if I was good enough for you. I asked you to be my wife, and you went to New Brunswick to look into my past."

Giselle sat on the couch and sobbed uncontrollably.

Tyson continued, "I offered you my love, and you couldn't give me your trust. Now because of you, my cousin is dead."

Giselle reached her shaking hand out to Tyson, "Please, Baby..."

Tyson turned his back, "Just leave."

Giselle checked into a Best Western Hotel on Route nine. After checking in, she snuck Buttons in inside her coat, praying all the way for his silence. He had been mewing incessantly in the car. Too late, Giselle realized she had left Button's pain medicine in Tyler's kitchen. She would have to return to her home to get his extra medication.

Once settled in she couldn't sleep. She missed the hard body which had warmed her so many nights. *All the chamomile in the world won't help tonight.*

Giselle slept fitfully that night and awoke the next morning to an ache between her thighs. *I miss him terribly.* How quickly she had become accustomed to Tyson's loving touches. Tears dropped onto her pillow as a weary loneliness set into her flesh.

After a light breakfast, Giselle called home hoping for a message from Tyson. There were three messages. The first was a long recording from a home improvement company; the second was Joe asking her to call the office immediately; the third was an unfamiliar, scratchy voice.

The third caller simply said, "I look forward to meeting you."

Giselle's body chilled. She sat holding the receiver long after the message ended. Giselle put the 'Do not disturb' sign on the door. *I can't have a maid finding Buttons.* She drove to her home and reentered through the backyard which had worked successfully with Mavis. The thought of Mavis saddened Giselle, but strengthened her resolve.

The blinds were closed, letting in only the softest light. She retrieved Buttons' medicine from her kitchen counter and tucked it into her pants pocket.

Again, hopefully, she checked her answering machine. The red light blinked feverishly. Giselle turned down the sound; then listened carefully. There were two messages.

The first was from Detective Chilly. "Ms Martin, please call me at your earliest opportunity regarding Mavis Love. You may reach me at ..."

Giselle pushed the 'save' button. The next message started. The scratchy voice said, "Do you know where your lover is?" The line went dead. Giselle sat heavily on the couch and shivered. She felt small and helpless. The police might have tapped her phone, but she had to risk a call to Tyson. Giselle hit the only speed dial number on her phone. Tyson's line rang ...and rang…and rang.

Disheartened, she crept to her front door to collect her growing pile of mail. She was about to go through it when she heard a car motor in front of her home. Peeking through the blinds, she spied Detective Chilly emerging from a white unmarked police car.

Juggling her mail in her arms, Giselle ran out her back door just as Detective Chilly rang her front bell. She returned to the hotel, parked in the back lot and went to her room.

When she finally calmed down, her thoughts turned to her mail. Amongst the junk mail and bills was a small rectangular package wrapped in brown paper. No return address, or any address for that matter, marked the package. In black marker the words 'OPEN NOW' were scrawled on the front.

With shaky fingers, Giselle tore the paper to reveal a copy of 'Windy roses'. Written in the inside cover in Tyson's neat handwriting were the words 'I'm glad you love me for myself'. A piece of loose leaf paper fell from between the pages. In the same scrawled lettering as on the wrapping it read, *'I know where your lover is. If you contact the police, you will love no more. Today at twelve noon come to the park bench where you saw me yesterday.'*

It was eleven o'clock. Giselle crushed Buttons' pain tablet and mixed it into his cat food in a saucer. He scoffed it up, making little smacking noises. When finished he curled up contentedly in the center of the unmade bed and fell asleep.

Giselle's mind raced faster than her car as she sped to the park. She easily spotted Tyler sporting a bright red designer jacket, sitting on the same bench where she last saw him. He leaned back seemingly relaxed, smoking a slim brown cigar. Giselle's spine tingled with adrenaline as she approached the sickly looking man. He smiled revealing gapped, discolored teeth which shot out at odd angles. What Giselle had earlier mistaken to be spiky twists was merely wild and uncombed hair. He looked out of place in his fashionable ensemble, as if someone else's head had been placed on a model's body.

"Well," Tyler said, "we finally meet."

Giselle recognized the, unfortunately now familiar, scratchy voice.

He gestured an invitation to sit with him.

Giselle sat gingerly on the very edge of the opposite end of the bench.

He continued, "You must be thrilled. You've waited so long to meet me."

"Where's Tyson?" Giselle asked with dread.

"Don't you want to get to know me better before we rush off? You were so curious about me before." He grinned a chilling piano toothed grin.

"What do you mean rush off? I agreed to meet you here."

"If you want to see Tyson, you'll have to come with me."

"I'll follow you in my car," she said hopelessly.

"I'm crazy, not stupid," Tyler sneered. His grin morphed into a grimace.

Two minutes later Giselle was riding in Tyler's cruddy Buick Century. The car was old, banged up and rusted. The interior was filled with fast food wrappers, old pizza boxes and empty beer cans, engulfing them in a land fill stench. The choking mixture included an ashtray overflowing with brown cigar butts.

Giselle cracked the window so she could take at least one decent breath.

Tyler jerked his head around, "What are you doing?" He glared threateningly.

"I can't breathe in here," Giselle stammered. She wanted to be brave like the heroines in her novels, but fear and confusion controlled her at the moment. *Am I crazy? Why did I get in this car? How do I know if Tyson's even alive? What am I going to do when we arrive? I'm no heroine.*

They drove over the Pulaski Skyway into Jersey City. After traveling through a maze of crowded narrow streets, they parked at the end of an almost deserted block. The only buildings in sight were abandoned warehouses. Litter floated down the street in the stifling hot breezes. They were in front of a dilapidated building bearing a well-worn sign, "Plumbing Factory". It portrayed pipes piled in haystack fashion.

Tyler got out of the car and walked around to Giselle's side. He jerked the door open and pulled her roughly from the seat.

They entered the rear door of the grimy, dusty mold green building. It was a one level warehouse with cement walls and dirt floors.

The few streams of sunlight which crept through the dirty windows highlighted the swirling dust in the air. Giselle tripped over a piece of rusted pipe.

"Look out," Tyler shouted. "There are rusty pipes all over the place. You're going to kill yourself before your time."

Giselle looked around with squinted eyes and finally spied a figure sitting in a chair in the far corner. As they drew closer, she could see Tyson tied to an old wooden chair. He was bloodied and beaten. His head hung forward limply. His torn Ralph Lauren polo shirt was maroon with blood. Long cuts covered his bare arms. He wore no shoes.

Giselle let out a little squeal, "Is he alive?" She

started to run to him, but Tyler held her firm.

"Yeah, he's alive…for now."

"What do you want from us?"

"I don't want anything from Tyson. He hasn't been a real brother to me for years, so I no longer care about or for him. What I want is you. He's was just a means to you. He's disposable."

Giselle quivered, "Why would you want me? You don't even know me." She watched Tyson from the corner of her eye, praying for even the slightest movement. There was none.

Tyler lit another cigar. Giselle crinkled her nose at the stench.

He moved closer and said, "You sought me out. Anyone who seeks me wants trouble." He loomed closer still, blowing the stinky smoke into Giselle's face. Then he walked over to Tyson's limp body.

He stood and studied him, then took a long drag on the cigar. Opening his mouth slightly, he inhaled the smoke through his large nostrils.

Giselle had a feeling of déjà vu.

Tyler suddenly leaned back and stretched his arms outward. With a hearty laugh he said, "This is the end for you." The smoky stench wafted up toward the ceiling.

Giselle bent and picked up a long, rusty pipe. She almost dropped the unexpected weight, but held on and swung as hard as she could. Tyler folded over from the force of the pipe in his soft belly. Smoke shot out of his mouth and nose.

Giselle pulled back and brought the pipe down on the back of his head. Tyler hit his knees, then fell forward in the dust. Blood gushed out of his head and neck. He lay still and moaning. Giselle swung one more time. No more moaning.

She rushed to Tyson and slapped his cheeks bringing him to consciousness.

Tyson mumbled, "Where am I?" He spied Tyler's broken body, now prone in a pool of his own blood mixed with dirt. "What happened to Tyler?"

Giselle untied Tyson's hands and feet. Then she lifted his face with both her hands and looked deep into his eyes. "It was either him or us, and we're what matter."

Giselle and Tyson walked hand in hand. The flashing police lights dotted the night like brightly colored stars.

Giselle held Tyson's hands in hers and looked into his eyes hopefully. "Is there any chance we'll get back together?"

Tyson looked at her thoughtfully and softly replied, "We'll have to work on the trust issues. I want to marry you, but your mistrust really hurt me. We can't have a relationship like that. We wouldn't survive."

"We will if you can just be yourself. No lines from books or movies. Just talk to me. Let me get to know you as you are."

"Maybe I should take some time to get to know myself before we get back together."

"I'll wait as long as I have to, Baby. I know you're the man for me and you're worth the wait."

Tyson smiled his warm, familiar smile. "I'm at a loss for words."

Bitterness imprisons life; love releases it.

Harry Emerson Fosdick (1878-1969)
Clergyman

SERITA'S SIGHT

Sitting in the sun, Serita almost felt normal. You know, like old times. Comfortable with herself. Rocking in that old wicker rocking chair on the porch with the warmth on her face. *Maybe I'm just napping.* Rock, rock. *Maybe I'm just daydreaming.* Rock. *Maybe I'm not blind after all.* Rock,rock. *Maybe if I open my eyes wide enough...* Serita stopped rocking, sighed, rose unsteadily and went inside. It had been two years since the collision, and sometimes she still forgot.

For the umpteenth time Serita evoked the night of the accident. Terrell was driving too fast. They swerved around the corner, charging an old oak tree disguised as death. Now she sometimes wished death had won the joust. Terrell escaped without a scratch, but the dashboard's head butt blinded Serita.

At first the doctors told her sight might return, but as time went on their words lost hope. Finally, their expectations evaporated.

Terrell and Serita stayed together four months after the accident, both knowing the relationship was over. Serita blamed Terrell for her blindness. Terrell shouldered the guilt until he couldn't watch her falter around anymore. One cool afternoon he vanished like the physicians' hopes.

Serita moped around for another six months. With the help of a home health aide, she learned the lessons of the blind, at least the physical ones. How to manage daily activities in her apartment. How to negotiate stairs, and cross the street. But Serita rarely crossed her own threshold and never the street. Even in the warmth of spring and summer she ventured no further than the front porch of her weather-beaten old house.

Serita missed her life. She missed parties, friends,

picnics, reading, movies, gardening, driving, but most of all she missed writing. Although unpublished, Serita had written for years. She wrote short stories, novels, poems, haiku, prose, essays, whatever entered her head. Before Terrell left, he bought Serita a voice activated word processing program for her computer. It was equipped with a speech synthesizer and screen reading program. All she had to do was speak, and it would type the words. She could then replay it and listen to her story. Serita used it once, but was heartbroken she could not peruse the pages visually. The computer sat idly from that day.

The ringing phone jarred Serita from her retrospection. "Hello?"

"Hi, it's your favorite brother."

"Glenn, you're my only brother," Serita sighed.

"I just wanted to talk. I haven't heard from you for a while."

"I've been busy."

"Really? Doing what? You never leave your house. You don't socialize with anyone. You're even more selfish than before..." Glenn hesitated.

"Go ahead. Say it. 'Before the accident.' Right?"

Glenn paused. Then quietly added, "Yeah, before the accident."

"It's about time you stopped tippy-toeing around me. Everyone thinks they should treat me with kid gloves, or I'll go crazy or something."

"We can't chance you hallucinating again like you did in the hospital. We care about you."

Quietly Serita said, "Yeah, the visions were scary. First I saw oak trees, their roots grabbing at my feet, the leaves smothering me, spitting acorns at me."

"Well, we know where that came from."

"Then I felt swirling quicksand sucking me under. I later found out they had given me hydrotherapy to calm me down."

"Then you had a choking problem?"

"The nurses gave me lemonade. The pulp felt like writing larvas. I spit it out all over them. I tried to tell the nurses about the larvas, but they didn't see them. They tied me down. It's really scary to have such tangible illusions. I never want to come unhinged again."

"We thought we lost you, Serita."

"Everything was so animated. I spent a whole week in the pysche ward, drugged up, never knowing night from day, or dreams from reality. Thank goodness, the doctors cleared my mind."

"That's why you should be grateful and enjoy life more."

Serita tensed, "That's easy for you to say. You can see."

"Now Sis, don't get angry. The family always stands by you. We shelter you more than you ever looked out for us."

"You think I'm selfish because I always fend for myself first, because I take care of me!"

"You always did, with no thought of anyone else."

"Well, I can't look after others now. If Terrell wasn't drunk that night…"

"If you hadn't let him drive that night..."

"I didn't feel like driving!"

"That's what I'm talking about. It's all about you. You never did treat him right. He gave you everything you ever wanted. All you gave him was a hard time. You just kept asking for more."

"What do you care about him? I've always been there for you."

"Oh yeah? How about when Sharon was sick, and we needed someone to watch the kids? You wouldn't answer your phone for two weeks. You knew we needed help."

"Oh, get off it. I have my own life to live. I didn't have time for that. If I'd wanted to raise kids, I'd have

had some. Besides, you never help me out. What about
when I needed a loan to pay my electric bill?"
"You hadn't paid back the last loan we gave you. Anyway, you spent your bill money on new boots, 'Miss Self-
sufficient'."
        "Why did you call here anyway?"
        "I wonder myself." Glenn hung up abruptly.
        Serita shook her head. *That's the story of my life.*
Nobody understands me.

        The next day Serita sat in her livingroom listening
to a guest speaker on public radio as he promoted the
skills of the handicapped and the triumph of the human
spirit.   He unfolded tales of individuals who had over-
come huge obstacles to achieve great goals. As he spoke
Serita fidgeted, tapped her nails on the dusty end table,
patted her foot, twirled her red hair and finally stood. She
flicked off the radio. Then slowly, cautiously, she crossed
the livingroom and clicked on her computer. The tower
hummed to life as if it had been turned off only an hour
instead of a year. Sitting at her desk, Serita felt around for
the microphone. It felt dusty. In fact everything on the
desk felt dusty. That damn aide. She doesn't do anything
around here. Serita opened her mouth to speak, then hesitated. What shall I write about? After a few thoughtful
moments, Serita concluded, *what better subject than myself?*
        She began. Serita regaled a tale of her wonderful,
pre-blind life and her sorrowful current existence. Tears
wet her cheeks as she inscribed her loneliness and heart-
ache. Serita saved the essay and went to bed. She fidgeted fitfully for an hour before sleep overtook her.
        The next morning as Serita rocked gently again on
the porch, she heard an annoyingly cheerful, "Hi there!"
        Gretchen McEvoy, Serita's overly jolly neighbor,
quick-stepped up to the porch and plopped down in the

wooden chair next to Serita's rocker. "How's it going, girl? I don't see much of you these days."

"Well, I don't get out like I used to."

"Why don't you come shopping with me sometimes? You must miss it."

"I don't like shopping anymore." *Can't she see I'm blind now?*

"You can't just be sitting around the house every-day? What have you been doing?"

Serita sighed, wishing Gretchen would just go to the mall, "I've been writing a little."

"Really? About what? Can I read some of your work?"

"No. It's personal."

After a prolonged silence, Gretchen murmured, "I guess everyone has a story." She sniffed and rose to leave. Her voice hitched, "Well, enjoy the day."

Serita hesitated, then reluctantly reached out, grabbed the hem of Gretchen's sweater and pulled her back into the chair, hard. "I'm sorry for being such a bitch. What's going on with you? Are you all right? Do you want to talk?"

Gretchen's tears flowed freely now. Between sniffles she said, "I need to talk to someone. You would never talk to me before, but I thought I'd try one more time."

"When did you want to talk?"

"Many times, but each time I approached you, you said you and Terrell had something to do."

Serita lowered her head and remained silent.

Gretchen continued, "After your accident, I came by a couple of times. I knew you were home, but you did-n't answer the door."

Serita hastened to change the subject, "What did you want to talk about?"

"Dan and I have split up. I just couldn't take it

anymore."

"Take what anymore?" Serita tilted her head toward Gretchen.

"The beatings."

Serita sat in stunned silence as Gretchen revealed the periodic beatings received from her drunken husband. They had started three weeks into the marriage. Dan wanted sex, but Gretchen was on her period. He had slammed her against the wall and stalked out the house back to the local bar. He returned. His arms were filled with flowers, his mouth with apologies. He blamed all actions on his inebriated state. She accepted her groom back with open arms.

A burnt dinner resulted in the next beating. Dan smashed their plates against the dining room wall. China shards sliced Gretchen's skin. Dan ignored Gretchen's spattered blood. She bandaged herself up and remained quiet. Each incident brought more fear into her life. Finally Gretchen gathered the nerve to approach the police for a restraining order. There she was informed Dan was a bigamist. He had three other wives each in a different state, each having filed restraining orders. The police in all three states were looking for him. Now caught, he was extradited to Utah for trial.

Serita offered the only help she could. She volunteered to listen whenever Gretchen wanted to talk. They hugged tightly, and Gretchen went on her way.

After Gretchen left, Serita sat silently a few minutes, then jumped up and went inside to her computer. *Now there's a story.* Settled at her computer, she began to write. While she wrote her head began to throb, but she persisted for two full hours until the story was complete.

The next morning Serita turned over, still half-dreaming of her beautiful blue bedroom. A gentle breeze billowed the white and blue flowered curtains. Blue petals floated featherlike from the curtains to the   floor.

Serita stretched sticking her foot out of the covers. She felt particularly good. She sat up and swung her feet to the floor. Her world blackened. *Wow. Did I sit up in my sleep? That was some dream.* Serita stretched again, smiling at her fancies. She rose and ambled to the bathroom.

Stepping carefully into the tub, Serita turned on the shower. She smiled as the steamy water sprayed her face needlelike. Suddenly each hot prick sparked lavalike lights off her skin. Bright orange splashes hit her legs. Serita gasped and backed against the cold tiles at the opposite end of the tub. Small golden waves of liquid heat ebbed and flowed over her toes. Screaming, Serita fell over the side of the tub onto the cold tile floor and fainted.

Hours later Serita awoke shivering. She lay in a fetal position on the bathroom floor. Her right ankle throbbed. She heard the shower still running, but the bathroom was chilled. Slowly Serita pulled herself up and shut off the now cold shower. She wrapped a bath towel around her quivering body and limped to her bedroom.

She curled up under her comforter and waited for her mind to calm and her body to warm. *Oh my god! Why am I hallucinating again? I thought that was past? I've got to get a grip, or they'll lock me up again.* Serita, eyes tightly shut, huddled in bed for hours.

By noon hunger had overtaken Serita. She gingerly arose from bed and dressed. Fifteen minutes later Serita carefully prepared to boil an egg. It was one of the few foods she trusted herself to prepare. As she lowered the egg into the boiling water with a tablespoon, the telephone jangled, causing her to drop the egg unceremoniously. She heard it crack as it hit the bottom of the pot. Cursing she grabbed the kitchen wall phone. "Who is this?"

"It's me, Glenn."

"What's up?" A few seconds passed. "Are you there?"

"Yeah. I have something to tell you."

"What's the matter?" Serita frowned, half because of Glenn's hesitation, half because of the egg.

"I just came from the doctor. I knew this might happen, but not so soon." His voice quavered. "I have lung cancer."

"W-w-what?" Serita stopped breathing.

"The doctors say I have six months to live. They can't do anything for me. I kept thinking I would give up smoking next year, or next month. I thought I had time."

"Oh Glenn." Serita's eyes filled with tears. With a lump in her throat she listened while Glenn recalled how he started smoking as a teen. Now in his thirties, he couldn't beat the nicotine cravings. Helplessly she spoke the soothing, but meaningless words we offer the terminally ill.

They closed with 'I love you's'.

The forgotten egg and pot burned and smoked. Serita dumped the pot into the sink and opened a window. She went to the porch, sat in her beloved rocker and cried her heart out.

At dusk, the doorbell rang. Gretchen entered, hugged Serita, and sat on the couch. "I wanted to thank you for listening to me yesterday. It meant a lot to me."

"No problem. I wish I could do more."

"Well, actually I was wondering if you would do me one more favor."

"Anything."

"Would you write my story? I want to send it to The Battered Women's Protection Society for their publication. They offer aid and information to women like me. I don't have the gift of expression you do. I know it's a lot to ask." She paused. "I'll understand if you won't do it."

"As a matter of fact, it's done. I wrote it last night. I hope you don't mind. You can have it. Copy it to a disk."

A delighted Gretchen eagerly copied the story to disk and left with her treasure.

The computer hummed soothingly while Serita sat thinking about Glenn. Hunger hit her again. She hadn't eaten since the night before. Walking into the kitchen, she jolted. Serita saw yellow. Yellow linoleum. *Oh please, no. I can't take this.* She shook her head in disbelief and shut her eyes tight. She opened them to see her old fashioned kitchen with the yellow wallpaper bordered with lemons and oranges she had picked out when she and Terrell first moved in. Serita took another step. As she did, the fruit began to fall from the wall and zigzag across the floor. The softly sunlit room began to fade. "No!" she screamed. "No! I want to see!" The scene faded to black.

As if it were her first day of blindness, Serita felt along the wall for the phone. She hit the Braille number three on the speed dial. A voice answered, "Dr Charles' office is closed. If this is an emergency, please stay on the line. If this is not an emergency..."

Serita held on until the answering service picked up. Then abruptly hung up. *Was this an illusion or real?* They could lock me up again. Serita leaned her back against the kitchen wall and slowly slid to the floor. She remained there all night.

The next morning Serita applied hot towels to her aching back. She refused to turn on the shower. *How am I going to keep it together today? I know. Writing will take my mind off of last night.*

After making a cup of Earl Grey tea, Serita settled in front of her computer. It was still on from last night. *What shall I write?* She drummed her fingers on the desk. *Of course, I'll write about Glenn.* She found the microphone and began. She wrote with tears streaming down her cheeks onto her tee shirt. Finishing three hours later, she called her brother.

"Glenn, how are you feeling?"

"As well as can be expected. I'm still reeling from the news, but I've decided to make the best of the rest of my life. It's funny, but when you know time is limited, you want your life to mean something. I've cried enough. Now I want prevent others from making my mistake. I thought about going to schools and reaching out to kids. I'd like to tell them smoking could change your life... or end it. I just don't know where to start."

"Let me help you start. I wrote your story last night. I'll forward it to you and maybe you can use it to get your foot in the door at the schools. Like an introduction."

"Serita, you're helping me? I mean, thank you. I'm going to need your support over the next months."

"I'll be there."

"I believe you will."

Late that afternoon, Serita leaned back in her favorite rocker on the porch. She closed her eyes and dwelled in a silent mixture of sadness and warmth. She opened her eyes and rose to go inside. *Ah the sun is setting. Wait a minute, I see the sun...and the trees and the grass.* Terror mounted.

Serita turned to run inside. Then she saw what could only be a mirage... Terrell. Everything grayed out.

Serita awoke to blackness. Someone moved about in her bedroom. She lay under the comforter, fully clothed except for her shoes. A cool washcloth soothed her forehead. "Who's there?" she muttered.

"It's me, Terrell."

"Oh my God," Serita whispered. "You weren't an illusion."

"A what?"

"When I saw you on the sidewalk, I thought you were a dream."

"You can see?" Terrell sat heavily on the side of the bed.

"I'm not sure. I thought I was going crazy." She relayed the past days events.

Terrell summarized, "So the first time you saw something was after you listened to Gretchen. The next time was after you gave her, her story. Then when helped Glenn, your vision returned again. Each time your sight lasted longer than before. Did you call your doctor?"

"No. I thought I was going crazy, but I'm going to call him now. You're no dream."

They both laughed awkwardly.

Dr Charles took Serita immediately and enthusiastically. After an hour of tests, he explained, "It seems whatever mental block you had before is breaking down. There was never anything physically wrong with your eyes. I don't know what's happened to give you flashes of sight, but whatever it is, keep doing it."

Back home, Terrell guided Serita to her favorite porch rocker. He sat down beside her and took her hand. "Serita, I came back to beg your forgiveness. I should never have left you, especially in your condition. It was terribly selfish of me. Can you ever forgive me?"

"Terrell, you don't have to ask. It's forgotten. I wasted the last two years of my life wallowing in self-pity. I allowed anger to swallow me whole. I wasn't living at all. I'm going to change that by giving to others. The last few days I've felt more alive than I have in years. The only thing I've done differently is to help others. I don't know how you put up with me all those years. I'm asking your forgiveness."

Terrell sat, mouth agape, for a few moments. Then he reached over and hugged Serita with all his strength. Serita gasped. The world lit up. Tears of joy washed the darkness from her eyes. She could see. It was all clear now.

ACKNOWLEDGEMENTS

I would like to thank my patient, encouraging husband, Tyris Henry, who critiqued my work honestly and always urged me to reach higher ground.

To my sister, Giselle—You've been my greatest cheerleader through all my endeavors. I love you very much.

Thank you, Family, for never losing faith in me in the years it took to produce my first book. Much love to you.

Joseph Campbell, President of BLACKNJ.COM , thank you for your guidance and generosity in many aspects of my career and for your never-ending friendship.

Moody Holiday, author, publisher, and writing mentor, thanks so much for the guidance you so unselfishly bestowed upon me.

Melissa Camacho, good friend and superb graphic designer, thank you for your observations and guidance.

Last, but never least, I'm forever grateful for my friends who waited patiently for my debut book and who, no matter what they thought, made me feel like a real author.

I love you all,
Gioya